NEEDLEWORK

NEEDLEWORK

First published in 2016 by
Little Island Books
7 Kenilworth Park
Dublin 6W
Ireland

ISBN: 978-1-910411-50-6

A British Library Cataloguing in Publication record for this book is available from the British Library.

Cover and end illustration designed by Stephen McCarthy
Insides designed and typeset by redrattledesign.com

Printed in Poland by Drukarnia Skleniarz

Little Island receives financial assistance from
The Arts Council/An Chomhairle Ealaíon and the Arts Council of Northern Ireland

10 9 8 7 6 5 4 3 2 1

NEEDLEWORK

DEIRDRE SULLIVAN

Little
Island

Acknowledgements

I have so many people I'm grateful for in my life. These are the ones who made *Needlework*'s journey a little easier.

To Diarmuid O'Brien, for being where my heart is – bright blue compass rose

To my mother Mary, my father Tim, my little brother Tadhg – hearts and anchors; the places that I come from keep me safe

To Gráinne Clear, Siobhán Parkinson and Jenny Duffy – a full-rigged ship with ladies at the helm, tall and proud

To Philippa Milnes-Smith – harpoon shining through the clouds, mid-voyage

To Dave Rudden, Sarah Griffin and Graham Tugwell – soft wild swallows guide me out to sea

To Ciara Banks and Suzanne Keaveney – the pin-ups on my shoulder, luck and love

To Claire Hennessy, Tara Flynn, Louise O'Neill, Anna Carey, Sheena Wilkinson, Sarah Crossan and Camille DeAngelis – mermaids on the rocks that sing encouragement

To Stephen McCarthy – the hand that guides the ink

To my students, guiding me to understand the complex world around us – a puzzle piece; a shower of bright stars

To the Office of letters of light, for Nanowrimo – a very welcome beacon

To survivors – safe passage through the storm; hold fast

For Nana (Alacoque) and Grandad (Mickey) Sullivan
I love you both

First prepare the skin. Not the room, the tools you'll use. The skin itself, a mental switch to open you to something. Tenderising meat, but in reverse. Prepare yourself for pain so that when it comes it is a good deal less than you imagined. Needles, things that fascinate me always. Much kinder and much crueller than are knives, a spindle-pierce through filaments and fingers.

A PRETTY STAIN
YOU CHOOSE TO KEEP INSIDE YOU

Mondays are Mondays. Eggs are eggs. Toast is toast. And once I've slung the gone-off eggs into the compost bin, toast is what I eat.

She is still in bed, eyes crusting over. She doesn't wipe it off unless there are visitors. Sleep lingers in the corners of her eyes, bright green and sometimes yellow-crusted pus. I want to pick it off but she flinches if I touch her even now.

She hates to be touched suddenly, my mother. I ask if she is getting up. She moans, although she knows I mean today and not right now. Her face is in the pillow and I don't know why I asked. I don't know why I even let my voice outside my mouth sometimes. There is no point to speaking. A useless flapping bird. A helpless thing. I knew she wouldn't move.

She works weekends. So do I, but one of us has school on top of that. The one of us that has school walks for the bus, stupid canvas shoes slapping into puddles on the way. Stupid feet that wore the stupid shoes. Stupid legs that grew the stupid feet. Stupid torso, shoulders and so on, right up all the length of me from toes to stupid head.

And that is how it goes until the bus stop. Which is also stupid. Can inanimate objects be stupid? Lifelessness just isn't quite the same. You wouldn't ask my shoes to take a test. Or the bus stop. Or even, when it does arrive, the bus, ploughing through the penny-coloured puddles of the morning like an optimistic beaver, looking for a place to build a dam. There is something flat-tailed and buck-toothed about this bus, which still has ashtrays and smells of them. Like Grandad's coat or certain people's fingernails at school.

I once painted my fingernails with yellow nail polish and when I took it off it looked like I had smoked with all my fingers. All of them at once. So far it's only two and only sometimes. I don't buy cigarettes myself, I can't afford to. I don't know how the bus maintains the habit.

The floor is always sticky and there is a lollipop that has been there since way before last week. Once upon a time it was lime-green. Or so the legend goes. Now it is mainly grey with specks of black. Fluffy as the mangiest of kittens. Clingy as the neediest koala. In my book, I draw a lollipop, the globe on it the eyeball of a cat. A shield composed of liquorice and fingers, an amber Chupa Chup containing ants. None of them look any good, not really. Maybe the cat one? It needs work though. Everything needs work.

A person can embroider any thing, a bag, a canvas – even a wall, I suppose. You do not need a thread, you know, not always. Not for embroidering skin. Colour. Needles. Eyes. The pain arrives with such specific delicacy.

Mondays are the worst.

I resent the lack of money earned here, where the work is harder than sandwich-making and weighing oily salads. More of it to do and less to gain. I'd rather do the laundry, shopping, taxes. Clean the windows even. All the things she can't find time to do. I find myself needing to spin minutes like a spider out of air – plotting graphs while sitting on the bus. Conjugating verbs aloud as I hoover the stairs. There's so much to a house. So many corners. All fill up with clutter and with dirt and no-one guts it out but me myself.

When I was small, I had a book of myths. I had a few but one of them had a fat grey cover and smelled a little off. Not like a book at all, but maybe spicy? I think it was my granny's as a child. I didn't like it, but I read it anyway. The stories lived inside. I had to know them.

Arachne was a weaver and she boasted. Women shouldn't boast. It's always a mistake for them to put themselves ahead of other folk. Or even, if you're Laura, on a par. People look to take you down a peg. To flatten you and stick a needle in. To feed you back your words and force them down your throat until you're sorry.

Arachne was a weaver and she boasted and she didn't praise Athena. Athena, boss of weaving. Other things as well. Goddesses had many hats in Greece. You know the way, in stories, sometimes people dress as other things to try and teach a lesson? Athena was an old, old woman and she said, 'Arachne, don't compare yourself to gods. It isn't right.' And Arachne didn't listen and kept going on about her weaving and maybe weaving was all she had, you know, because there wasn't very much else about her in the old grey book I had with the matte cover.

So, Athena showed them who she was, revealed herself, and staged a weaving contest. Of course she won. She wove a lovely tapestry of gods, the different ways that gods have punished mortals who stepped up above their station.

Laura is like that, she makes her point and then makes it again and makes it five times. I think she likes that she can have one now. A point, I mean. (She could before, but not so very often. Not when Dad was in the house as well.)

Arachne was weaving too. My friend Anna, when someone's being brave, will say they have 'brass ovaries'.

It's gross, but you could say that about Arachne. She wove all the shit things gods have done to mortals. Zeus, chief among them. Zeus was rotten. Turned in to a swan to rape a woman. I'd rather fuck a man than fuck a swan. Even non-consensually. I mean, a swan. You'd never see it coming.

Athena saw the work, the pictures, and she got mad and ripped it all to shreds. Arachne was invested in her art and when it was destroyed that broke her heart and she went home and then she hung herself.

This book, now that I think about it, could not have been for children. Who'd want that kind of thing for a bedtime story?

When Athena saw the body, she felt bad and gave Arachne back her life, but as a spider. Cursed to do the thing she loved for always. Cursed or blessed, depending on how nice you think gods are. I always went with cursed. I'm quite predictable.

Stitches that the doctors make are ugly, artless things. Purposeful and all too often clumsy. When I think of needling at skin, I think of colour. Embroidery might not be the right word, although there is no right and wrong to thoughts unspoken.

Illustration, then, with pen and ink.

Irish. Gaeilge. First class. Grammar exercises, while the teacher looks through other grammar exercises. The ones we were supposed to do for homework. It's not what we do always. Sometimes she makes us *comhrá* – like, chat to each other. Doesn't go down well. I try my best. I don't like talking even when it's in a proper language, one that people use.

I don't always find time to do my homework. I intend to, but things get in the way. Which is a lie. Well, not a lie exactly but not the full whole truth of it either. It sounds better than 'I get too exhausted.' Teachers hate that young people get tired. We should be bags of verve and hormones. We should always be able to do more than we did before or are currently doing.

My nails look rotten. Ratted skin around the edges of them that I can't seem to stop picking at, even when there's blood. The little white fronds seem so ripe for sloughing, I peel them off like wallpaper that hurts. My hands don't look like I want them to. They're stubby, lined and leathery as bags. I like the way they draw. How deft they are at putting things together. That's about it, though.

I'm OK at Irish sometimes, although I feel like my tongue is too ungainly to wrap around the words the way that it is supposed to do if I want to be understood. It's the having to do things that I don't like, piles and piles of things I have to do, oozing up to cover me like quicksand.

Pulling me down, I mean. Heavy's how I feel with each new task.

Which is not good, as Mondays are my weekend. My break from work. Twenty hours a week in the stupid newsagent's beside my house. Two full days and one late-night shift a week to keep us going. They always give me more, though, in the end. And if I don't comply, I lose the hours I need. The money's supposed to be for school things, clothes and books. Most of it ends up being spent on groceries. She has a job too, in the museum. Telling people things and so on. It's twenty hours a week as well, which you'd think would mean she'd clean the house and cook most of the dinners. You'd be wrong.

Your needle is a pen, and ink your pigment. Fish-scale silver, saucy ketchup red. Mute or lurid colour. A whisper or a scream.

When I get home from school she's still in bed. She won't get up unless she has a reason. I'm not a reason. Just another chore she's putting off. A bit like homework. I should do my homework. But there's so much else to do besides, like mow the lawn, or put bleach in the toilet. Hoover. Unblock sinks. Draw things in the margins of my textbooks. Laugh, cry, scream, kiss, touch, breathe. Brush hair, brush teeth, brush floor.

Grooming the house as though it were a person or a horse. I will not live in filth. I get embarrassed by it, even though I don't have people over, wouldn't have them even if it sparkled. Embarrassed for myself. I am ashamed to live the way I live, I suppose or guess. Or something. Is that strange?

You can make skin glow secretly at night-time. A constellation just beneath the surface, appearing like the moon when it gets dark. This is fairly new and hard to come by. But tattoos are old as ages. I would like to make things beautiful, but a tawdry and repulsive kind of beauty. A braver sort than people have from birth. Sexy pin-up zombies on a bicep. That sort of thing. I'd like to get it right.

Tom's house is messier than ours, but for some reason I find the squalor there relaxing. No rules, no dinners to make, no cleaning to do. And they have a trampoline in the kitchen. Not one of the little ones. A big one. They stole it from next door one drunken night and now have no idea how to return it without admitting fault. Meanwhile, the kids next door to them have no trampoline and have taken to jumping sadly on the front lawn on an imaginary one their daddy made them out of lies.

The boys also have a fort made of beer cans in their living room. They had to move the television to allow for an extension to the east wing. Tom and his friends are ridiculously proud of their little fort. To the point of sometimes sleeping in it, in spite of there being one too many beds in the house.

Tom's friends are like that, though: they have adventures. All been friends since school and like each other and support each other. I've never had that and I'm kind of glad. I don't think I would want it at the moment. People knowing things can creep me out.

I like sleeping at Tom's because he has a double bed. I've never slept a whole night there, not once – but sometimes I'll cat-nap, when I take a day off, which is hardly ever. Also, the sheets don't smell like me at Tom's. I don't know what I smell like, but a different smell is safer, somehow – sort-of.

I like the way Tom smells; it makes me feel better. I'm not sure about what, exactly. Not about my relationship with Tom, which is kind of ill-defined. There is something very wrong with it, amoral even. Not on my part, or on his, but kind of both. I'm using him while also being used.

Not that we don't get on, we do. But I wouldn't call it love. Sometimes, I wouldn't even call it like. But there are times I might – maybe – call it 'a thing'. If I'm in a romantic frame of mind. I haven't decided if it is definitely a thing. And whether, if it were a thing, it would be a good thing or a bad one.

There's a right way and a wrong way, Granny said, her fingers looping wool around a bobbin. In this old world. A right way and a wrong. I'd like to get it right. With this I think I'd like to get it right.

The learning that we do in school astounds me. So many leaves unfurl from curly buds. Or not. I think I would rather be doing almost anything than sitting here, than talking to my friends, than eating lunch, than learning even more.

I'd love to take a nap. All I want to do right now is sleep. I'd love just once to spindle-prick my finger on a curse and drift off for a hundred blameless years. Or maybe more, I wouldn't really mind.

Laura once told me that in the old fairy tale, the sleeping beauty before 'Sleeping Beauty', it was not a kiss that woke the princess up, but sex. I nodded, like, 'That'd do it.'

She shouldn't say those things. She should pretend that none of it exists and not just utilise the parts that suit her. She is my mother after all, and aren't mams supposed to be like Barbie dolls, all smooth and sexless except when there are babies to be made?

I think I'd rather the slumber-curse itself than the breaking of it. We're not supposed to *not* want to have sex. It's this mysterious thing that nobody has done or not done. Though from the way the girls go on about it, you'd swear it was an injection that makes you cool. Instantly sexy because somebody wants to have sex with you. A woman.

Prancing around saying things like *Do I look different? I feel different*, and other things like that. This is why I keep myself quite private. Not that I don't have friends. Not that I don't talk. But never the full story.

For instance, they get an edited version of Tom. Laura, my mam, knows a little bit about him. Me and the boy next door. Isn't it adorable? If she could see what we get up to, she wouldn't think so. Not that I want her to see what we get up to. But maybe to worry? To be engaged with me, and want me to be safe and warm and cared for and not treated like a child or a real doll, depending on his mood. I amn't sure which mood I prefer. I'd like something in between the two, I think. A real child, or an ordinary doll. Or just, you know, a person. Sometimes I would settle for a person.

You need to bite your lip and swallow down the part of you that doesn't like the sound of people hurting. The little breaths, the tiny beads of blood. The part of you that hates to leave a mark or be remembered. This thing right here. This thing in several seconds' time will be indelible. A thing that you have done that will stay put.

The week after we moved into the new house (I use the term 'new' lightly; I use the term 'house' lightly – it is mostly made of plywood and fag ash, and the landlord never fixes anything and the smell of drink off him), I started doing stuff with Tom. Not, like, right away. We did talk first. That's how it began. Normally that's how these things begin. You say things and look at each other.

At least I think. I've never had a boyfriend before. I suppose that he's my boyfriend-thing. Or something. Except I'd never call him that, not in earshot. I'm not sure whether or not that's childish. Like, ewww boys! I try to be *blasé*. *Blasé* is quite an adult thing to be. Mostly because of the *aigu*. Children don't know much about *aigu*s. They'd probably call them *fada*s, like in Irish.

Children (the ones with proper childhoods anyway) don't have fuck-buddies either. Which is closest to what Tom is to me, really. More of the boy, less of the friend. More of the benefits less of the friendship. Or only enough of it to keep the benefits coming. And that's kind of both of us. But there are times when friendship seems like it would be a benefit as well. I'd like to have somebody beneficial. In my life.

The room itself must be hygienic, tools as clean as babies' unborn teeth. Wrapped in meat and waiting to be smiled. Hands pristine, piercings covered, hair inside a net. All in readiness.

There is love and there is like and then there is compulsion. I don't know what it was exactly that kept my mam and dad together all those years. Sometimes I wonder if it was me. My birthday is six months after their wedding anniversary.

She used to love saying *Not in front of the child*, to delay a row, not that it always worked but there were times it did. It wasn't for my benefit, just a way to claw back some control.

I don't really get the whole not-in-front-of-the-child business anyway. Just because it is not in front of the child doesn't mean the child can't smell, see, hear or taste it. Sight is only one of all the senses. I always assumed that another one was thought. The ability to reason and deduce things. What is that if it is not a sense?

You need to know about skin. And you need to know about ink. And you need to know about hygiene, tools and people. The simple things that keep a person safe. The dermis is the meat of the skin sandwich. The place you want to hit and fill with ink. Above it wouldn't stick and under it, you'd probably do damage. If it seems like it's a lot, don't worry. Most of it is sense. Breathe out. Breathe in.

In chemistry I draw the symbol for alcohol. Ethanol, I mean.

$$H{-}\underset{\underset{H}{|}}{\overset{\overset{H}{|}}{C}}{-}\underset{\underset{H}{|}}{\overset{\overset{H}{|}}{C}}{-}O^{\,H}$$

It would make a boring tattoo in black and white but maybe with the right amount of colour? Bright like jewels the inks that you would need. Not dull like pens. I always have a pen in every colour. To make things easier to read again.

In the margin of my book I draw a wizard with the face of Dmitri Mendeleev. He has kind eyes, but his beard has caught on fire. He shouldn't have let it drift so close to that candle I drew underneath his beard.

My eye hurts. I think that there is an eyelash in it. I don't want to poke my eye with my finger because that looks inattentive. In maths, the teacher keeps asking me questions, really pointedly. As though I were a dunce. I don't know any of the answers. Trigonometry is hard.

I draw a cone of glass with a D on it piercing an anatomically correct heart. Aorta, *vena cava*, ventricles and everything.

I love the way the human body looks in textbooks. Disgusting and beautiful. I have some physiology books that I picked up in this charity shop the week we first moved in. You could look at them for ages. I've been copying some of them in my sketchpad. Trying to get them all exactly right.

You have to be able to draw stuff accurately. Because people want their tattoo to be exactly the way it looks in their head or on a printout that they give you and why shouldn't they want that? It's a forever thing that's painful and expensive.

I have a mole on my right calf, which I hate because calves are one of the weirdest shaped parts of the body and the mole kind of accentuates the fact that I have calves. But I would miss it if it got removed because it is a bit of me, though not by choice.

I change my mind a lot about my flaws. Sometimes the mole seems very small and other times it's big and so disgusting.

When I am older I will have more choices. And more money. And more time. And a double bed of my very, very own. And I am going to be happy there, with no-one but myself to give me grief. Older is a place I'd like to go right now. But I don't have the skills to live there yet. I need my mam. But I don't have a mam like other people. I just have Laura who is in no shape to be human.

And when the skin arrives it will be lovely. Smooth and soft and pitted with its pores.

This is my earliest memory. I am on a beach and I am small. There is sun-cream in my eyes and it is mixed with sand and I am crying. I am wearing a ridiculous sun-bonnet and it has a lacy brim and it is white and cotton, maybe linen. The elastic on it bites my head and I can feel my skin burning and I'm not sure whether it is anger or heat that does it but it is scaring me.

Mam is trying to wash out my eyes with 7Up because there is no water. Salt water would have hurt but so did this. Laura's stupid logic, even then. Later, she gives me an ice-cream sandwich out of guilt. Angry still, I hurl it on the ground. She slaps me on the face and makes me put it in the bin. I have to go on tippy toe. The bin is full of wasps and I am scared.

Unprepared skin poses a problem, twinges, quivers – maybe even squeals.

I think about this in home economics class as we mix the dough for the brown bread we are making. It is challenging to make a perfect loaf of brown bread, apparently. It is when you don't have the ingredients and have to scrounge the butter, milk and flour from your more organised classmates, who resent the favour. I can tell they do.

I am not liked. People who do not know me automatically assume that I am a cold bitch. That is the phrase they use. Maybe it is true. I find it difficult to warm to people. I always assume that they pose a threat and gird myself accordingly.

I don't think I am cold, though. Deep, deep down

I think I'm all too warm. A hot and stupid hedgehog, spongy as fresh dough beneath my spikes. I would like to be different. I would like for things to have been different for me. Almost everything. My hands feel sick with butter that I use to grease the tin. Bits of dough still cling to them like warts.

While the bread bakes we write the recipe into our copy-books. I think of a picture: a whipped ice-cream cone, pristinely perfect peaking off the wafer. A single wasp alighted on the side, getting ready to nestle in and ruin it. The wasp is the loveliest thing about it, though – the gold and black belly, the big bug eyes and gauzy little wings. The sting.

Kneading the dough requires a light touch. There is nothing light at all about our dumpy little teacher, with her scarlet mouth and designer handbags. Her husband is a dentist, which is why she drives the nicest car in the school car-park. I read somewhere that dentists have the highest rate of suicide among professionals. Then psychiatrists, after that accountants. Decay lurks everywhere, threatening their pearly white existence.

I wonder what the suicide rate is for people who work part-time at deli counters. Someone probably knows, has graphed it in relation to sandwich-induced disgust.

It is hard to hate sandwiches and go to school. Everyone is constantly eating them. With their stupid, dentist-killing teeth. I would never kill myself. That's not to say I don't want to die the odd time. Sometimes I fantasise about never having existed or fading into air a little at a time and one day just being gone. Not missing – just not there. I'd want the memories of me to be gone as well, though, because herself would use it as another 'oh, poor me' story to go on about on the days when she doesn't feel like getting off the couch or out of bed. She calls them 'pyjama days', as though it were normal for her to have them.

Tom and his friends have days where they skip out on class and hang around the house too, but those are different. Less self-pity and more boldness, doing stuff they'd not be allowed to get away with at home. I think it is OK when you are in your first year of college to do a bit of that. Acceptable laziness. When you are forty-three, though, it's not okay anymore. Not when you have a daughter. She says that she is depressed, but she shouldn't be, not any more. I'm not. I wouldn't give him the satisfaction.

That's the thing with skin. It's not a canvas or a cloth.

I was born with a face on me. This is why people stay away from me. I can see why. My face in repose is sullen. My lower lip full, my upper lip thin. My eyes are grey and my nose is what Mam calls aristocratic. You can see the inside of my nose because my nostrils curl up a bit. I have to clean my nose more than a normal person because anything that lurks in there is visible. Also, I have decent skin and eyebrows that think I am better than you, in spite of common sense. I'm not unfriendly, but my voice is kind of low. Surly. I don't go up and down like other people. I rarely squeak.

So, make sure they're sure before you can begin. As sure as sure can be.

At school, I keep my head down, do my work and largely go unnoticed. I have what I suppose you would call friends, a group that I eat lunch with, talk to and so on. Most of what I do to them is listening, though. They don't know me. They know the girl I show them. The me who is not me but looks like me.

I came easily to the group and now I fit in, like a coin that sits with all the other coins in a tacky slot machine, the one with the light-up pirates. What I mean is that alone I stick out but with them I am camouflaged. They don't ask many questions. People like to talk about themselves. They know about my job, my school before and some things about Tom. This is enough.

I think for me that would also be enough. Would make

things simpler, clearer. More definite. Pure as water, I could flow through life if things were just as simple as I tell them. Days and weeks and months have passed since first I came here, obvious and slow. Nervous and alone. Eating my wrap, I am glad to be assimilated.

Then lick your chops and set yourself to work.

It is night. I don't have to be quiet or pretend that I'm asleep. Mam is out, so no-one's here to notice. The cars and talk and cats and bins and everything outside are pooling in my ears, waiting to be digested, put in boxes. Grey noise washing over me to sleep.

The new house is grimy, a shabby clone of all the other houses in this estate. The area in which we live is cheap, full of students and foreigners and other folk who live their lives on budgets. I am sick of budgeting, I think, as the cracks on the ceiling form a heart, a tree, a charted constellation – stars and lines. I am sick of checks and balances, pros and cons.

Con: Things are bad

Pro: Things are better than they were

I can feel my eyes begin to droop and the last coherent thought that I remember as I drift away is this: *Am I happy?* When I wake up I still don't think I know. I could be, sometimes. Maybe. Never in the dark.

A BRUISING LITTLE ETCH

Things I draw are these:

A girl, eyes big as two-euro coins in her face, holding a
scabbard like it was a sword
A hand outlined – fingers splayed inelegantly – and the
shadow that it casts
A traditional heart with flowers, doves and arrow – the
scroll inside it reads 'anyone'

Brush my hair. Ponytail. Teeth. Eyes. Knickers. Tights.
Bra. Uniform. Moisturiser (hand cream). Bag. Lunch
(packed). Breakfast. Check on herself. She is home but
tired. Kiss her on the cheek and out the door.

My nail polish is chipping and it looks cheap. Shoddy.
Sitting on the bus, listening to the Walkman Mam got
me in a charity shop. I'm hoping to pass it off as a hipster
thing and not a broke thing. I am the only person I know
who has a Walkman. I like it, though, the wall of sound

between the world and me. I don't even need the music to build that wall, it's like a gift I have. I can sit and filter out and not even be aware of who I am or what is going on around or inside of me.

It's one of the things I trained myself to do when I was little. That and hopscotch. You're in your body but you're far away as well. You cannot feel the things that you are feeling. It isn't you. It is another girl. You close your eyes and focus on not being where you are. Think of colours, flowing under skin. Waves of ink-blood swirling into flowers, branches, hearts.

Music helps to start the inner drift. A softer version now, for walks and home and buses. I'm not here, but I can clean the toilet and the windows. A robot who remembers where she is.

Music when I study helps me focus, the hum of everything replaced with noise. I like to do as well as I can on things, not that it'll get stuck up on the fridge or anything. I won't be able to afford to go to college, probably. Even with free fees and whatever grants I'd be entitled to. I don't think I am entitled to anything much, though, seeing as Dad earns a decent enough salary. Well, not like banker-huge, but fat enough. He gives us money every now and then. So he can say he is to other people. Doing the right thing.

She'll take his money if they go to court. Whenever

that's a thing. She has to wait for years to get divorced, but they could get a legal separation. 'It's still a recent thing,' she says when I ask her. 'I don't want to rush into anything.'

I ask her if they will get back together.

'No, but ...'

I ask her what the but means.

'I don't want *her* to win,' she says, and that's the end of that.

Not that I want to go to college, but I'd like to know that I could if I wanted to. I mean, I could go where Tom goes, live at home and that could be a thing. More money. More hard work. To avoid feeling inferior when everyone I know moves one way and I move in another. So, that's why I study, even though I don't have that much time.

A tear in skin is not usually something that remains. Impermanent. It takes a lot to scar. You must go deep. People think of skin as something simple but in fact it's intricate and layered. Puff pastry made of flesh. Folds of ancient lace, stiff, dry and pitted.

I'm on a late tonight, which can be horrible or lovely, depending on the customers. Type and volume. I like to be really busy, or not busy at all, so I can get on with other stuff. Once the stock is replenished and faced off, and the floor and counters are cleaned. Facing off is pulling products to the front of shelves, turning all the labels right way out. Putting a good face on it. Pretending like there's loads of them behind. That it's OK. People like to see things being normal.

You don't have to go to college to be a tattooist, but I'd like to know more about art and stuff, the background and techniques. I don't really know anyone who is one. I think you get an apprenticeship for a couple of years. I think Japan, the States or even London would be good places to learn the trade.

I have my own home-made machine, but I'd never use it on anyone, myself included, because it isn't properly sterile. Also the ink I can afford is horrible stuff. I wouldn't draw on anybody with it. Well, maybe Dad. I can think of a few choice words that would complement his forehead rather nicely. His forehead or his fists or hands or crotch. The horrid bits. The eyes. The mouth. The brain.

The inks I want are the proper ones you use for Japanese body art, the bright rich colours of jewels and Christmas shop-fronts. The kind that will not require touch-ups for years and years. You have to get practice skin, but you can't get that around where I live. Laura's credit card is used for things that Laura wants to buy. And if I stole from her, she wouldn't like it. I'm mad at her a lot, but she's my mother. The last best hope for someone to depend on. So I just use pig skin that the butcher beside the shop I work in sells me. It's cheaper, and closer to the real thing.

The only problem is that after a while it begins to stink. That sounds as if I've done it loads, but I haven't. It takes me ages to design a tattoo, and ink is so expensive, even cheap ink. I want to do it more, though. I want to get really very good.

I take pictures of my work on Mam's old camera, which she is looking for and I have stolen. If she knew I had it, she'd go mad, but I think that she is only looking for it because she thinks I have it. The camera on my phone is broken. Something happened to the lens before Laura passed it on to me. It's crap and cheap. Only there to ring when she needs me.

This is how you scar. Heat or cold will do it, steel or laser light. You can flay the flesh, or brand it like a beast's. Early artists used a form of this to do their work, it is more refined now, the sliced skin patterns rubbed with ink or charcoal. Pack it in and do not pick the scabs.

How you make your own tattoo machine is this:

The first thing you do is to collect a shed-load of stuff. I got this list off of the Internet, and I don't think it is the only way you can make one, but it worked for me:

an electric toothbrush, batteries, ruler, wire cutters, guitar string and a lighter.

You need some bleach inside a little bowl. Bleach, they say, or hydrogen peroxide. It's the same thing. It's just another name. The chemical formula for hydrogen peroxide is H_2O_2. Just a 2 from water. That seems like such a little difference, but it's big. Drinking bleach can kill you. Duh, I know. But isn't it strange how little tiny differences on paper can be significant and threatening when they trip off the page and into life?

Take Dad, for example. Not much difference between him and another person's dad on paper. Socks and sandals, jeans and shirts and, sometimes, woolly jumpers. But there was something lacking. Or extra. Something small, but in him from the start, and it rippled out of him and touched both me and Mam and now there's something wrong with us as well. Something un-bleachable, and the sticky grey of it colours us both – damaged, warped and wrong.

Next you need soap, hand sanitiser. Gloves. Big, sterile cotton pads. And superglue. Q-tips and a marker. Obviously, ink. I only have the cheap kind. Really, I should be using medical-grade stuff. But it's not like I'm doing it on people. The pig skin doesn't mind. Maybe if it were a whole pig my work would impact, I'd save and save and fork out for the extra.

Indian ink, the black kind of it anyway, is made from

soot at first, I read somewhere one time. I wish I could make it out of the ash in the stupid fireplace. Mam can light fires, but she never cleans the grate out. I have to do it all, all by myself. It is strange how much ash a fire makes. You think of them as destructive things but what they leave behind is a new something, so in a way they're creators as well. Sometimes I wish I could set bits of myself on fire and turn them into pure bright ash that looks like something else completely. When something is burned up, it's hard to tell exactly what it was before the fire. It is a secret thing, unreadable and tricky to decipher. I feel like I began from soot as well, from something dirty. I think that if I burned into your skin, you'd get infected, swell with yellow pus and get a greenish scab. It would be the kind you shouldn't pick but really feel like picking. It would be the kind that leaves an ugly scar.

You'll also need disposable containers.

Once you have all these things, you will feel pretty pleased with yourself. You shouldn't, though, because your work has just begun.

You break the toothbrush just right, add a bit of wire-cut guitar string. If you want it extra sharp you should cut it diagonally. If it's blunt, you have to be all stabby, and even though people (Mam) go on and on about masochism and pain addiction in relation to tattooing, people who are being drawn on with needles mostly do not want to be in agony. The sharper the needle is, the less pain there will be. The machine is now almost ready.

Place the needle in the blue part of the flame to purify it. Hold it there for three to five seconds. It actually looks beautiful. There is something a bit hypnotic about fire, when you stare into it – a beautiful, hurting thing. A poison-snake.

I must design some snake tattoos. Their skin is really pretty. My father's mother has a snakeskin bag. She once said, 'You can have that when you're older.' She meant it at the time. Not so much now. I'd like to touch a snake that was alive some time. I think it would be cool.

Pour the bleach into a small dish. (I used an ashtray, but I cleaned it first.) Leave the needle in the bleach for around five minutes. This is to sterilise it more. If something is going to bite through your skin, it should be cleaner than clean. It is important. You need to wash your hands, with a nail-brush, properly. Including the webs between your fingers, thoroughly scrubbing thumbs and wrists. Shake your hands to dry them, like a dog, or use a towel that has not been used before. Sanitise your hands. Only then put on the latex gloves.

Remove the needle from the bowl of bleach and place it on a sterile cotton pad by way of drying. Glue it on the metal tip of the toothbrush. As it dries, please hold the needle straight.

When all is ready, the tattoo should first be gently traced on the skin with a non-toxic, non-permanent marker. Put the inks you want into separate sterile containers. Unwrap the tattoo machine. Turn it on.

The needle should pulsate up and down rapidly. Place it in the ink. Trace the needle over your design with the machine. Take your time, and be as light as possible in your touching. It's not your job to penetrate the skin. Leave that to the needle you have crafted. When you are finished, allow the lines you drew with marker to fade away, leaving something lasting in their place.

This is oddly satisfying. I imagine it will be more so when the skin is actually affixed to a person. Or a pig. Wouldn't a tattoo look funny on a pig? I wonder what I would put on one. Probably a heart with 'Sty, sweet sty' or 'Sows' in it. A friendly little Garda. I wonder when the word 'pig' began to be used as an insult. My money'd be on chimpanzee for the animal that most resembles an ugly human, though. Filthy creatures, chimps. And violent too. I've seen a documentary.

Undue irritation ruins the pattern. If done right the beauty can appal.

Mam told me this story once, she'd heard it from her grandmother, who swore it really happened. What it is, is this:

There was a wealthy publican who lived in a big and fancy house just outside the little town where my great-gran grew up and he had a wife and she was beautiful, a bird-like thing with wispy bones and hair. They were happy together as two people who have nothing to be greedy for can be, but they had no taste for the aesthetically unpleasant things in life. One night there was a storm that split the skies. The kind of storm that everyone remembers – a tree-bending shriek of a thing.

And in the middle of the storm there came a knock upon the door. Now, the publican and his wife were both at home, for it was Sunday and he was a god-fearing pillar of a man. Also she was heavily with child and he wanted to take care of her, because she was so delicate and fey. Had she been poor, she would probably have died while still a baby, people used to say. But she was rich, and lived.

But when he answered the door to find a Traveller woman and her squalling brat, he was annoyed at being so disturbed. She wanted shelter, and he was about to let her in, when his wife came to the door, asking what the noise was. She wrinkled her nose and looked away, and he knew that the woman's presence made her uncomfortable. So, while it wasn't exactly what he wanted to do, he told the woman to leave his property. She begged him to help her, held her baby to his face. It was an ugly little thing, smelling of shit and turf fires. His wife looked between two minds. It was a horrid night, and the baby was exceptionally small. But he did not back down, and when the woman refused to leave, he got irate, called her a sow, her child a suckling-pig. They never saw her or her baby after the night of the storm.

But when their child was born, slimy and raw with its mother's meats and fluids, they had a big surprise. Once the caul was stripped away from its infant head, the baby's face was seen. It was that of a pig. Not just the snout, but eyes and mouth and bristly little face.

They decided it had died at birth and put it somewhere. Or so the story went. They bought his poorer brother's youngest baby. Never had a litter of their own.

I don't think that it is true. I've heard that story since in other places. With little changes, the moral stays the same. Don't cross a tinker woman or you will be sorry. Granny called them tinkers when she told it, Mam sometimes too. The word feels wrong inside my mouth, though, now.

Livia, my friend who works the register when I am on the deli, knew a girl who saw a Traveller woman shoplifting, and called security on her. The woman was annoyed and told her that she would be very sorry. And when Livia's friend's baby was born it had the face of a pig.

Not really. What really happened was that they waited after work to beat her up. She ended up in hospital. (There's something, isn't there, to these old tales? A message.) But *anyone* could have beaten her up really. It wasn't because the woman was a Traveller. That comes out of the way they tell it. All you need in order to have a gang and beat somebody up is violent friends.

When I listen, I don't contradict, I nod my head. Let people hate on other people. It isn't my problem, as long as they don't hate me. I can't take any more hate or love. I feel I'm fat with the wrong sort of both.

Ink is not the only thing you can pack into a wound to warp its healing. Mud and ash can do the job as well. Your magic skin will find a way to force out foreign bodies. Some even use the ashes of their dead. The scars left by this method are raised and angry, like childish stick-on wounds at Hallowe'en.

This is what myself and Livia talk about as we dust and fill and organise the shelves. I slice ham for tomorrow, and think about Tom. The ham slicer is a scary machine, a horror waiting to happen. Since working here I have heard tales of fingers, elbows, hair and nails, things caught and trapped and severed. When the purpose of a thing is to slice meat, using it brings home that meat is also, essentially, what we are all composed of. It growls and whirrs ominously, like some sort of mythical beast that creeps into your room at night, bent on slicing delicate young skin.

To leave a pattern but to avoid infection is a challenge.
You do not want the skin to heal too badly or too well. Acidic
juice can be used to prolong the irritation. If you don't have
some human ash to hand.

I have drawn monsters in my notebook, some from stories, some that I've made up. There are a lot of legendary beasts that live on people's skin but not in the real world: gryphons, unicorns, dragons, phoenixes, salamanders, nymphs. Isn't it strange how many people recognise make-believe animals before they do the ones that actually exist? Sawfish, sea dragons and sugar gliders sound fabricated somehow, but they're not. I saw them in a book. *My Australian Picturebook*, which at the moment provides my night-time reading. It is a bit pathetic, but the illustrations are something else, really, really lovely – kind of grainy and old-fashioned, but in a good way. All the animals in Australia look vaguely suspicious. Especially the marsupials.

Marsupials are all over the place in Australia. I'd like to visit there some day if I ever have enough money. If I ever get out of this place. So many ifs. I sometimes see my life as a series of doors shutting loudly, one after another. It's my own fault, really. We'd have more money if we lived with Dad still, and I was the one who pushed for Mam to leave him. I convinced myself, if she took that step, all the reasons we have to hate each other would melt away and things would be better. And they are, except I hate us both.

Anything can grow from people's skin. You can slice out squares of skin to form a mosaic or a tree. Spines become trellises for ivy, stars appear to litter someone's arms. Your ribcage can become a net that heaves with freshly caught fish, open-eyed and gasping.

She is seeing someone, this man called Simon, who is in insurance. They are having lasagne and watching a DVD at home tonight, and I have been told to make myself scarce. Which would be fine, except that I am angry with Tom.

Here's why. On my way home from school, I had an hour to kill before I went to work, so I texted him to see if I could call over. He told me that he was not at home, which is OK. Except for the fact that he was, I saw him on my way to work, sitting on the sofa with the curtains open, playing Xbox. Tom plays a lot of Xbox. This is probably why I am the first girl he has ever gotten physical with.

The strange thing is, he doesn't even care about me much. I always thought people who didn't have people to hook up with had, like, this whole discerning thing going on, where they were choosier than average and had standards and stuff. I thought it was a cute sign that I was his first. I mean that is what one would think. I'm not completely out of line.

He should count himself lucky that I like him that way at all. He totally doesn't, though. Which is fine, because he's not my boyfriend. I don't owe him anything and he doesn't owe me anything. Except for maybe respect? I would like some of that, please.

Anyway, once the meat slicer is clean I start covering stuff up with Clingfilm. I still have about two hours of homework to do, but I can't do it at home because of the sex noises. The stupid walls are tissue-paper thin. It is kind of horrible and wrong. I wish I didn't care about any of it, Mam and Simon, who is OK really. He is the first boyfriend she has had since Dad, and Dad kind of didn't count as a boyfriend because he wasn't very nice to her at all. Last month, Simon bought me a birthday card. It had a fifty in it.

Mam was all 'Oh, you shouldn't have,' but she was glad he did, because it meant she didn't have to give me any herself. She bought me some second-hand encyclopaedias, a yellow jumper and a book about mutants. She is a good mother, or she can be. It's just that she is broken and she knows I am as well but that doesn't stop her breaking me even more.

I don't know what to do to fix my mother. I'm trying but I always seem to end up hating her, or yelling at her. The first night I stayed over at Tom's, when I got home she slapped me across the face. I think that she was jealous that I was doing something normal, when she can't remember how to be her normal self any more. Not normal the way she was growing up, anyway. Granny and Grandad were pretty well-to-do, you see. So Mam is kind of used to better things. Things like a clean house and a shower that isn't just a tube connected to the taps in the bath.

I never feel clean after a shower in our stupid house. I always feel like I still have a smell hanging on me. The shower in Tom's is electric, so there's always hot water, and the flow is pretty strong. I should probably not hold it against him, the whole ignoring-me thing. He did it once in town as well. I said 'Hi!' and he walked right past me, like I was a stranger.

I asked him about it and he claimed he didn't see me. He did, though, I saw him see me. I didn't bother arguing. He is not important enough to hurt my feelings. I am only using him for his amenities. I'm still not going to call over tonight, though. Because, even though I know we are kind of using each other, I am feeling vulnerable about things, and I don't want to be with anyone.

I wish I had my own place to live, away from Mam. Maybe near enough to visit and make sure she doesn't do herself an injury or something. I worry about that sometimes. I wonder if she worries about me, she doesn't appear to. I'd ask her, but that would totally make her worry. I'll be OK. I'm good at coping with things, I can handle pressure really well. I've always been able to, I suppose because I've always had to.

In the metal basin, flesh collects. The little scoops you took to ridge the skin will soon be placed in little yellow bags and disposed of.

School today was hard. I found it really difficult to keep my eyes open, particularly during maths class. The more I tried to stay awake, the sleepier I got. I think I drifted off, because my head bobbed a bit and the next thing I remember is Joanne elbowing me under the table. It must have been really obvious too, because my head did the whole bobbing, drooping and then jerking up thing. Ugh. Not that I'm worried about how I look or what people think of me or anything, but I must have looked like a right fool. Because of this I have no idea how to do the homework.

I was kind of hoping Tom would help me. He did honours maths last year so it's not like it'd be a big stretch or whatever. Can't ask him now, though, because of how he's being. I'm so tired all the time these days, almost too tired to sleep, if that makes any sense. And when I do sleep, I have these dreams that aren't exactly nightmares but still feel really vivid and terrifying.

Like I dreamt that I was growing wings at breakfast and the feathers kept on falling into my cereal and all of a sudden my mouth was full of feathers and every word I said was a crow-black river of them, covering the table. Mam just kept on wiping them up, sweeping them onto the floor with her hands. I wasn't wearing shoes, and so I stayed at the table for a long time, staring at the feathers and the milk. When you wet a feather, it loses a lot of its beauty, its shape changes and warps into this little stringy thing, like mangy sets of eyelashes, back to back.

Mam likes false eyelashes, because her natural hair colour is this pale, pale ice-blond. In the sunlight, her brows and lashes are almost invisible. I was scared of them when I was small, worried that, like spiders, they'd crawl into her eyes and lay their eggs there and when the babies hatched, Mam would go blind.

You must be careful with the flesh of others, it can hold so many dangers. Pretty scars seem like deceitful things, weaving glamour into pain, unconscious of the dangers.

I had a very vivid imagination when I was a child. I used to become scared of household objects. There was this chair in the sitting room, one of those fake leather ones, and it was really cosy to sit in, you would kind of sink down into it as though it were a granny's lap. Shortly after my eighth birthday I became convinced that the chair was capable of eating human beings. And what's more, that it had designs on my delicious child's body. From then on I would not sit on the chair and whenever I had to spend time in the sitting room, I'd eye it warily and count the steps I'd need to reach the door. Seven or less and I would feel content. Any more and my spine would fizz with readiness to bolt.

I hated that chair as much as Dad loved it. I can still picture him in it, watching the football or whatever was on telly, tie loosened, belly pressing softly at his waistband. The day of my eighth birthday, Mam had made a cake. She let it burn and so he held her hand against the stove until she screamed. I was wearing a new dress, with a silly Peter-Pan-type collar. It was purple and Dad had bought it for me. I preferred my jeans, because there would be games and things. The colour was OK, though – purple was my favourite colour at the time, it still is one of them – but this dress was the wispy, lavender-mauvish purple that isn't really much of a colour at all.

My cousins came over and there were kids from school as well. I don't really remember who except for Shane Horan. I kissed him on the mouth and then gave him a Chinese burn so hard he cried. I was a strange little child. I still am, in a lot of ways, that girl. I'll spend the most intimate of moments in Tom's arms and after that I'll roll out of bed and back to my house, drawing a pair of spectacles around his eyes with markers by way of a goodbye. He said the time I did that hurt his feelings. In my defence, though, he was fast asleep.

There is a bit of the bully in me, but I don't know which side I get it from, because Mam has a lot of it in her as well. She told me it was my fault, sometimes, when bad things used to happen. That I caused it somehow, by not doing or by doing things she thought I should or shouldn't do. She made me scared as well. Everyone I come from can be scary and I will be that way when I grow up and that is scary too. I can't have kids. I'll never have a child. I won't have children. In case I'd be like Laura or my father.

Karo women bearing many scars in Ethiopia. They represent the woman's age and status. There is one in my encyclopaedia and she is smiling. Bumps all down her tummy curve. Like the prints you do with cotton buds in primary school. Pointillism.

There is no magic spell to change a person, though. She couldn't make me into the daughter that she wanted. I couldn't make her happier, or my father less cruel. I didn't really think of him as cruel, though, not all the time. Because he would do nice things too, like buying that dress for me or throwing me up in the air and swinging me around and around until I was sick with the fun of it.

He told me stories about when he was small, the bold things that he did in school. I found it hard to believe that he had ever been bold while he was telling me those stories, but other times he was the boldest ever.

Bolder than Shane Horan, the boldest boy in my primary-school class, the one who stuck a pencil up Maria Feeney's nose and it got stuck and she had to go to the doctor and when he saw she got off school he stuck a pencil up his own nose too, but his mam couldn't come to pick him up for ages, so he had to sit by the door with a bright red wooden cylinder protruding from his left nostril for hours and hours. Nobody laughed at him, though, because if you laughed at him he'd not forget but wait his chance and hurt you in some way.

I wonder what happened to him. Where he came from, what kind of home he had. We used to talk about who would win, in fights between our dads. I remember telling him my dad would have, if Shane's dad made him snap.

I said this proudly, like it was a cool thing that he did.

'My dad snaps as well,' he said.

But not like mine. I knew I was the winner.

I wonder if he ever thought about that later, or if it

was normal for him too, to have a dad like that. It wasn't normal, though. Not by a long shot.

Some tribes do it to their children young. Prepare them for the pain in life ahead. On flat ground, under trees. Tenderly. It's hard for us to watch but comes from love. Inner scars are harder to admire or respect. You cannot fathom anybody's pain with just two eyes. The things they've done the things that they will do. Drawing bracelets round their wrists with rusted nails they've found in garden sheds, clear as a scream. But muffled things are harder to decipher, living in the marrow of your bones. Fragments of them claw at guts and brains. How does anybody sleep at night invisible?

I have the worst headache walking home from work. And when I walk past Tom's, he waves at me through the window, ushering me in. He makes me a toasted sandwich in the kitchen. I hate sandwiches but I am hungry and it is a nice thing for him to do. I wolf it down. He smiles at me across the table.

'You sound like a pig eating from a trough,' he says and I look at his face, trying to read it as a joke. It isn't one, though. We both know that it isn't one.

As he sleeps, his face is child-like, all the meanness gone.

When I leave his room, homework still neglected, to

go back home for sleep, I think about what he meant. Why he said that, after doing something nice for me. My stomach seems to bulge over my waistband, to prove him right. I pinch a wodge of skin. I wonder if I could slice it off, stretch it out and fashion it to canvas for my wonderful machine? I know I couldn't. In the dark I rake my nails down the soft skin of my inner arms – elbow to wrist.

It was Shane who taught me this game first. There is a proper story that goes with it, see, and the trick is to surprise them with the hurt.

The story's this: There was a red man and he had a little red wife and they had a little red daughter, but she moved away. The little red couple wanted to go on a walk to their little red daughter's house, but all the roads were grey and much too hard for their little red feet to walk upon with safety. They needed a red road for their red car so they asked a girl/boy to build one for them. And s/he did.

As you tell the story, make gestures on their hand, to illustrate the tale. Their arm should be bare and prone, all innocence and waiting for your scratch. That is how you play red road. Until I sleep I play it by myself. There was a little red man and his little red wife. They had a little red daughter, but she moved away …

The kind of hurt you pay for

Sailors had the right idea really. Needles in your body show you're tough. When you go places, you should remember somehow. When you come back from travels, people see the marks on you and ask.

At breakfast Simon asks me how I am. I'm full of snot, but say that I'm OK. Mam looks on as Simon pats my head on his way out. She holds him in the hall, their voices murmur softly. I leave through the back door, not to intrude. Mam gets hugged so little. There is something inside of everyone that craves affection. I have touch hunger, but also touch disgust.

I woke alone in a cold bed, feeling like a whore. Long sleeves this morning. It is a cold day, the kind of cold that seems like it will be warm enough until you step outside. The sun looks lemon-yellow through the clouds. They say you shouldn't look at it directly. Or you will lose your sight. They say a lot of things, though, so sometimes there is too much to remember. *Brush your teeth after every meal. Just ignore them. Before you cross look right and left and right again once more. Eat your vegetables.*

At the bus stop, an older man tells me to cheer up and give him a smile. How dare he presume to make me change my mood to suit him. I glare at him, and pointedly I blow my dripping nose. I am coming down with something. This is a good thing, because, if it's a bad one, I'll rest and lose some weight. I can skip school for illness, but not work.

Amulets and stamps. Those marks on you, they speak a secret language. A swallow was five thousand miles at sea. And two was ten. And on and on like that. A swallow is a lucky, flitty bird. It zaps around the sky so small and elegant. The confidence of swallows. The shape of them, the little feathered thought to calm and ground you. To bring you home when you have travelled long.

Today I find I'm desperately sad. My head is heavy and my body slow. Everything's a trial. Even conversation. Joanne has had a row with her mam about some thing we're going to on Friday. I tell her that the world isn't ending. Everyone is rowing with their mam. We're full of feelings, women. We boil over.

I think that Mam was mad at me this morning. Cold snake eyes, his hand upon my head. She didn't like that, and I know just why. I must not tell her of my row with Tom. Not that it is a proper quarrel, even. He will be fine – unless I make a fuss. Tom doesn't like a fuss. He calls it drama. As if my grievances are all an act. And in a way they are. I find it so hard to care about anything at all, that sometimes I have to force myself to be offended when he does some things I do not like.

I would like affection without strings but that's impossible. You don't even get that from mother love, which people go on about as if it's somehow sacred. This sea of love and loyalty mothers have, this so-poetic thing that blesses us, that makes us who we are. My mother loves me, but there are conditions. Each time her life becomes more difficult, or I act out in some way, ties are snipped. She hugs me sometimes, crying. What would she do without me? Without me, would she have stayed with Dad?

An anchor for safe passage on the Atlantic ocean. Underneath you'd write a thing that grounds you. Mother. Father. Wife. Ink and paper. Safety. Books. A place you love and hope you will return to.

Here's another story from the book. My granny's spicy book I called it once to Mam, or so she tells me. Laura's stories from when I was small revolve around my cuteness or my boldness. Glossing over all with sheen of glib.

A monster met a woman and they had a baby. The baby was half a monster but it was the hidden half, the half below. During the day, she could disguise this half. At night she bathed her scaly legs and tail in secret. When she met a man, all she asked was that he leave her by herself to bathe. Of course this man could not resist the breaking of taboos. He stole outside her window and espied her deformity. The shock filled him with anger.

With a tweezers, he pulled out her canines. They were fangs. They'd been fangs all along. He saw that now.

With a razor, he shaved off her scales.

With a sword he docked her of her tail.

Naked and bleeding, she was thrown outside. Her eyes were dull. She had expected this.

The lot of monsters isn't very happy. I draw an angry eye inside my book. A woman made of snakes. A crown of bones upon a kingly head. A woman holding up a mirror to her decapitated neck. A jar of honey filled with many bees. I am very tired.

Geography is mostly about stones. The types of stones, the types of things they make. Features of the landscape. When you look at things like that, you kind of assume they have been there for ever. They haven't, though. Things erode and shift, they form and fall.

But what you want's a turtle or a dragon. The equator. Oriental places. The orient sounds so exotic now. Joanne, who was adopted from China, says to call it 'orient' is racist. I don't know why. I like the sound it makes, the pictures in my head. Fine silks and smoke and long thin beards. And dignity and cherry-blossom trees and opium. I kind of see it now. I shall move on.

Dad hasn't given Mam any money this month. 'My money' is what she calls it. As if she is entitled to it. As if she's earned it. Maybe you could argue that she has. I don't want anything from him at all, but she thinks she deserves it. Maybe that's why she's so edgy.

The teacher has a moustache. Not a small one either. It is hard to look her in the face. It's badger-grey, and almost kind of pretty. I wonder if she sees it on herself. It is kinder to tell a person these things, I think. Unless it's something they can't change in a trice. Panty line and hair where hair should not be are easier to sort than fat or acne.

Joanne is great at taking people down a peg. Not ever to their faces. Which makes it better, I think. Not so cruel. She's smooth and she's together. Big pores on her face are always clean and her hair smoothed back is bumpless. She's stuck so fast together I don't think that she'll ever come apart. I keep my mouth shut, though, when I notice people's flaws because it always seems to come out meaner than I mean it. Harder.

A star if you had gone around the Cape. Small and blue behind your ear. A full-rigged ship could signify the same. That you had braved the worst of it and lived.

Dad used to pick on Mam's looks a lot. Never mine. That's one of the things that Mam resents. That Dad fancied me and not her. Fucked up as that is. I think that's why I don't like to cuddle Tom in the dark. Or sleep beside him.

God, I hate my life. I thought Dad was the source of all my problems. And now he is removed and things remain the same inside my head. I wish my brain was metamorphic rock. Dark blue limestone changed to purest marble, wiping clean the dirt that lurks in pores. Like a phoenix, rising from the heat, all new and perfect. Innocent as babies in their cots.

Last night I dreamt the feather dream again. This time my screaming filled the room right up until it was a soft black pool to drown in. Sinking, I was worried for the birds. All those feathers have to come from somewhere. Even in my dreams they don't materialise just out of nothing. In an adjoining room there might be crow after crow, undignified and plucked. Without feathers, wings don't work as well. You clip the wings of pet birds so they cannot escape. All the crows that couldn't get away were in a room beside me, desperately cawing. I woke up to a pillow wet with tears.

Halfway through Irish, I begin to daydream about escaping this place, not by becoming a lawyer or a doctor or whatever, but by physically removing myself from the situation I find myself in right now. The purpose of my escape would be simple – sleep. I would find a place where I could go to sleep, and then I would sleep there.

There are not a lot of places to sleep if you don't have any money and are dodgy about appearing to be homeless. Toilets, but public toilets are generally disgusting. They smell and are made of cheap, hard stuffs: plywood, plastic, metal. You taste things as well when you breathe them in. I try not to think about that too much, though. School toilets are OK, as toilets go, but I think somebody would notice my teeth grinding and slumping and it would draw talk. I do like the hiding-in-plain-sight element of being in the school, yet not at school. I wish there was a small janitorial closet featuring a bed that I could happen upon and no-one else would ever find but me.

I begin embroidering this fantasy: brushed cotton bedclothes, a small but powerful radiator that actually works (the ones in our classrooms are for decorative purposes only), a kettle, even? Why the hell not? This is my daydream. Ooh, and a huge deadbolt on the door, so I could shut everybody out and not have to deal with any of it, none of it at all, until I'm ready.

Two crossed anchors, coolest one of all, meant that you had sailed the seven seas.

Mam does not approve of daughters locking doors. She likes to poke around my room for evidence of any damage to my psyche she can find. Not with a view to helping, mind. She just likes to yell at me about any secrets she uncovers and finds suspect. She hates my book of drawings, thinks it means I'm gone beyond repair. The pictures in my head jar and perturb her. She'd much prefer I kept them bottled up. An eye inside a bottle drowning in formaldehyde.

I could hide my sketchbook from her, but she would worry and begin to ferret and unearth. I don't want her to know about my hiding place. Underneath the floor of my dodgy wardrobe is a hollow. It is there that I keep my machine.

When we first moved in, I found the skeleton of a bird inside it, and also a small amount of weed. The weed I sold to somebody at work. I sprayed the bird skeleton with antiseptic stuff and left it in there. It is kind of amazing, almost weightless. Birds have hollow bones to help them fly. Lacy-light are their skeletons. The one I found was polished to an almost eerie sheen. Obviously loved and touched a lot. This was, at first, a good deal unsettling to me but now I see the point. It is very comforting to look at. How complex we all are. Even the little things that dip and flap. I think the bones may once have been a crow. Initially I thought a starling, but then I remembered that feathers and flesh would bulk up the thing a great deal. I wonder what size my skeleton would be?

There was a giant man once who lived where Granny Kate lived, way before her. He had a morbid fear of doctors stealing interesting bodies. Well, not in general. His specific case, his flesh and bones. He was right to be fearful. They stole his corpse as soon as he was dead. Some folk believe you cannot get to heaven if your body is desecrated, not buried in hallowed ground. I think that can't be right. Although I'm sure there isn't any God. I learned that for a fact when I was small.

A gold hoop glinting through the pink meat of your earlobe paid for burial if you washed up on the shore. A good idea, if a little morbid. It mattered, though, you see. Sailors were a most religious lot. Saints and crucifixes. Talismans. Protection. Anything to save them from the sea.

I almost had a little brother once. But then my mother

did something to Dad and he got angry. It could have been a dinner that got cold, or burned. It could have been a mutter or a kiss. A look upon her face, even.

Anyway, I was outside. In the garden, in my Wendy house, with my group of seven favourite dolls. The guild of dolls. My dolls were angry with me. Their eyes were beady and I was calming them down by offering them cups of tea. I had pulled one of their arms off the day before and they were quite bitter about that. My dolls were a very strong unit. I was the boss, but they always sided with each other when there was a grievance. I remember being really, really scared that one of them would pull my arm off.

I was waiting until I was called for dinner. I knew it would be any minute now. Usually we ate around half six, and while I couldn't tell the time yet, I was pretty good at knowing when it was almost dinner-time. My tummy started to rumble as I poured the dolls a second cup of invisible tea. Mam had promised to sew Blue Doll's arm back on. My dolls never had definite names, they changed with the seasons, or what I liked to watch on the TV.

Dinner was late, and I knew that Dad would be angry. It was a rule that I had to play outside till I was called. Not when it was raining, but normally I had to wait for dinner to be ready. When dinner was ready Mam would let me know. I was hungry, waiting with the dolls. It got dark, and darker, darkest ever. I was cold and hungry. Too hungry to wait. But when I tried the back door, it was locked. Pale-faced, I went back to my Wendy house. My dolls laughed at me. They told me that my mam and dad had gone away for ever and that I would have to live outside with them (the dolls) and do what they said.

I walked around the house, the car was gone. On the road, I saw a drop of blood. I knew what blood looked like because I had seen it before, when I cut my knee and got a bandage that had Winnie-the-Pooh on it at school. And other times. At home, our bandages had no-one on them. They were the kind of colour that tries to be skin, but isn't really skin. You know the one. And when you rubbed them, they were rough like cloth, not smooth like plastic. I made my dolls into a sort of blanket-bed for me. They were not happy, but I was sick of making them happy or unhappy. They would do whatever I said and just shut their traps about it, because I was cold.

It was dark and I wiped the blood off on Blue Doll, just where her arm had been. I wondered what had happened, if Mam had cut her knee or something. I didn't really think she'd cut her knee. I worried she was dead. All night I worried she was dead, until Dad came home and unlocked the back door. He was hungry and wanted a sandwich and a cup of tea. I made one for myself while I was at it. It was my first cup of tea, and it was hot and

I felt like a grown-up, drinking tea with Dad. He had a packet of chocolate digestives, and between the two of us we ate them all. He didn't tuck me in that night, and all the blood – there was more inside the bathroom when I went – had disappeared by morning.

Next day, instead of going to school, I visited Mam and spent the day buying her things from the hospital shop. We didn't have a childminder for me, she had to do it even when she was sick. Mam had to do a lot. Mam made sacrifices to keep me safe and happy, you see. She still does even now, or so she says.

HOLD FAST. Bold and big, remind you just what you need to do when the ship tosses wildly in a storm. Hold tight. Hold fast, and don't let go until you really have to. Fast means tight as well as meaning quick. I suppose you'd want them both inside a crisis. Speed and strength like Superman or God.

Mam called a mouth a trap sometimes; she still does. *Shut your trap* when I say something cheeky, or offensive. A mouth can be a trap, that much is true. A woman's mouth especially. Tom has told me I have a mouth on me, on more than one occasion. As if it were a bad thing. As if I shouldn't really have a mouth. Which is ridiculous when you think about it. People need mouths. For eating and for talking. Things that women are ashamed to do, too little or too much. An ill-kept mouth is a dreadful thing. Rot can set in so easily. If you eat sweets. The words that you say can also cause the rot of friendships.

That's why I'm quiet with Joanne. Anna was my main friend from before. I unfriended her when we moved here. Unfriended her and blocked her. I don't want the taint of it on me. We're not that far from where it all went down. I mean, it is another town, but close enough to get there in an hour. The place where I grew up. Mam and me both wanted to escape. Not have it at us.

She once said to me, 'I cannot bear the thought of him with her.'

She never calls the other woman Breda. She calls her 'her' or 'that one', 'bitch' or 'it'. As if she took a happy thing and broke it. As if we didn't need to go before.

Pig on left knee, rooster on right foot. They cannot swim and live in wooden crates when they are cargo. Save you from a shipwreck, make the current float you to the shore alive and gasping. Roosters good at fighting too. Make you vicious, jabbing for the eyes when in a pinch.

I like to be quiet, but not too quiet. A mystery. No-one can solve me, although sometimes I think Tom would like to try. Just to say he had. There is something strange in him. I do not know if he is a cruel person who pretends to be kind, or a kind person with flashes of cruelty. It doesn't matter. What I need him for is simple. My stupid heart, though, sometimes disagrees.

What is it about touch that bonds a person to another person? I think about it sometimes, but not often, as I try to keep me on the surface, skating over every rotten thing. If I opened my mouth, disastrous things could happen. I'd scream you deaf, I'd gobble up the world.

Once upon a time there was a little red girl in a little red house, where she lived all alone. One day she found a little red river, and decided to follow it. When it got dark, she tried to go back home, but red is hard to see when it gets dark. She sat on her little red bottom and tried to have a little red cry for herself, but no tears came. It was too dark for tears.

I hate that, when you think that you could cry but are not able. There is a release in tears that people need. Laughter too. I used to laugh at Mam when she fell down, silly Mam. It wasn't that I meant it to be mean. It was the scaredest laughter ever, but she looks at me sometimes like she remembers, like deep down I am mean, I am like him. I wonder if she's right.

Everybody mostly wants to live. Or if they don't they want to choose the time and maybe method. Twin propellers

scratched into your bum that nudged you to the shore if you
submerged. A lot of things to bring you safe to shore. If they
liked shore so much, why did they sail?

My hands at the bus stop are icy fists. So cold that they
are warm. It is five o'clock and there is no bus yet. My toes
feel like my fingers. I wore two pairs of tights today, but
it does not seem to have made any difference. I have so
much, so many things to do.

Miss McManus is retiring. We have to bring in a tenner.
I do not have a tenner to bring in, but I pretend that I
resent the note demanding money because Miss McManus
is a bitch. She is, but I would be too after twenty years of
teaching. We have her for religion. Sometimes she just lets
us do our homework. Once, when I had trouble reading
her writing on the board, she snapped at me that I should
get some glasses. There are pros and there are cons.

I kind of resent parting with my hard-earned money
for Miss McManus's benefit. She probably makes more of
it than we do put together. The electricity bill is coming
soon. We got cut off before, back at the old house that
we shared with Dad. He let it happen, just to show he
could. How helpless we were without his big fat pockets.
He liked to drive that home every now and then. There
were good things about him too, though, he was good at
fixing stuff like me. He had a nice singing voice. We have

the same ridiculous sense of humour. I am aware of these things. Also, I have his mother's bony frame, not big and soft like poor dead Granny Kate. I'm like the other one. My fancy gran. The smart one who wears heels and gets her nails done. The one who doesn't speak to us at all.

'You get that from your father's side,' says Laura when she's angry.

But I only have a few, those little traits. Is that enough? I want that to be enough, no more of him in me. I'd slice it all away if I'd survive.

When you travel, sometimes there is death. No matter where you are. But for old-timey sailors it was common. People drowned or drifted or got stabbed. And you remembered them with drawings on your body. A swallow, pierced upon a little knife. The one of you who died. The fallen comrade.

I'm so tired that I fall asleep on the bus and end up having to walk home from the terminus. Forty minutes of rainfall.

As I walk past, I get a call from Tom to come over.

'Come over, love,' he says. And so I do. He calls a lot of people love. Women in shops who give him things. People on the phone. It doesn't mean he loves me.

He has something to say, but he forgets what it is, as I peel off my wet clothes. My uniform spins in the dryer and like a cat, he licks me clean as clean. My homework undone, I shower and watch television with him on the couch. He flicks through the Internet on his laptop, avoiding essays or whatever it is that he is supposed to be doing. He is always complaining about having stuff to do, but I've never really seen him do a tap of work. He doesn't have a job. I put my head on his shoulder like a girl in a film. I like doing this, because it feels normal. Or as good as. Like it could be somebody else's life.

The sitting room smells of boys. There are four pairs of runners beside the couch and a poster of some film I haven't seen on the wall. It looks like it is about fighting. And possibly drugs. The artwork is quite nice, but I would have made the lettering more ornate and the shadows rounder.

There is a man who has a cat tattooed upon his torso. Its back is turned to you and his navel is its puckered little bottom. Tom finds him on the Internet for me. I almost spit my tea into its cup.

'He must really like cats,' I observe.

The picture is strange, well drawn. But why would someone do that?

'For attention or a laugh, I suppose,' says Tom, but it disturbs me.

When I get a tattoo it will be something private and meaningful. I would like my life to have privacy and meaning. I suppose the cat-bellied man has other priorities. Laughter. Sex with cats.

The boys that my Tom lives with are quite nice. They're friendly, like. They make me cups of tea the odd time. Ask me how I am and tell me things. I used to see them more, before we hooked up properly. I'd call around to Tom's to watch a movie. To be normal. And then the sex. So that's what we do now. And it is fine, but sometimes I miss the other, friendly moments. Watching them be pirates on the Xbox. Listening to music. Smoking things and laughing on the couch.

Tom thinks tattoos are cool, but he doesn't know anything about them, or understand why they hold my interest so much. I don't tell him about my plans or anything. We don't have that kind of relationship. He is talking about this girl he knows who has put on weight. He thinks that she should stop eating because she used to be cute and now she looks too thick around the middle. I wonder if he's talking about me. Trying to be subtle. We don't have a weighing scales in our house, my trousers aren't too tight or anything, but still there is a contempt in his voice and I'm afraid that it is meant for me. It could be meant for me. He is not the most subtle colour in the palette, though, so probably not.

I wonder what Tom would be, if he were a colour. The navy of his tracksuit pants. The black of his hoodie. There are shades that I associate with him, but he is not one colour. Try as I might I cannot pick the colour of him out.

Goodbye and home, because he is going somewhere. Some college thing. He walks me to my door as though he were a gentleman. As though I were a lady. I fumble with the keys as he walks off.

Memento Mori is what those are called. Like in the old days bracelets made of hair, brooches with a tooth in, photos where your corpse is standing up with loved ones as though it still were quick. I love Victoriana on the Internet. The morbid little ways that people cope. I'd like a list of them, to know them all. I have a few that work for me but maybe there are better ones to try. Nobody's dead but I keep losing people.

When I get home I do my English questions first, while my brain is still rested. Mam is in her room, but doesn't want to be disturbed. At the kitchen table, I wait for my pasta to boil and do my English. Add the sauce and then attempt my maths. I finish them. I take some up to Mam. She doesn't want it but she says she'll eat it. I go downstairs and then I wash the saucepan and the bowl. For vegetables and dessert I eat three apples while I do my Irish. It is late by now. My hair feels tangled. If I don't brush it out after a shower, it weaves into a single wiry mass.

I didn't want to do it around Tom, shed like a dog all over his house. Traces of me mingling with the mud and hair and skin that fill his carpets. He doesn't mind that I am on his sheets so much, but this is kind of different. Nothing pretty about clumps of hair. Not that it would have made much of a difference, but I know he would have been annoyed if he had noticed.

I trust him with some things, though. Bit by bit. Light stuff before the heavy. Like Robert at work says about weight-lifting. You start out small and bit by bit then you can handle more. I do share stuff. I do. I'm not a robot. I sometimes wish I were.

Sailors didn't go in for funeral jewellery. They committed to missing people that were gone. To missing them forever with their skin. I like that. It is kind to miss a friend. And there should be more kindness in forever. Etched into biceps, scrawled upon your shoulder-blades and back.

My throat hurts. I am coming down with something. I make a hot whiskey with lemon and honey. One for me and one for Mam. This she gratefully accepts. I sip it as I do the final thing. A diagram of the human heart. It seems easy, but I keep on getting side-tracked. I draw a perfect model, but it is tiny and black as coal. Then another one of crystal glass. All whites and blues. *If it beats too hard, this heart will shatter* is what the legend underneath it says. It would look nice in special shining ink. The glowing kind that brightens in the dark. Transparent things are hard to draw because of the light refracting on and in them. Then on the graph paper side of my science copy I draw and label the proper one. What I'm supposed to do.

During the night, I blow my nose almost constantly. There isn't room for sleep, I'd drown in phlegm. At some point in the night, I turn my alarm clock off deliberately. Knowing I will not be woken up will help me sleep. It is cold in my room. My bed never seems to warm up until the morning time when I have to leave it. Life is miserably unfair that way. I wonder how many days of school I've missed. Not too many. I think that you are allowed a certain number before you get in trouble. Mam hates me missing school, because she worries that people will think that she is an unfit mother, that they'll take me away and give me back to Dad. I don't think that it works quite like that, but I don't really know. Maybe if I get a doctor's cert? Maybe then she'd let me stay asleep.

I am so tired. Underneath the wardrobe, I imagine my bird and my machine, asleep as well. The gentle whirrs and caws their snores would be. What would I do, if one or both of them came alive all of a sudden? The bird would fly away, if it still could. But my machine would be my little pet because I made it. I would feed it ink and blood and it would sterilise itself, by growing a little tongue and producing anti-bacterial saliva. Is saliva anti-bacterial anyway? I read somewhere that's why dogs lick their wounds. My small machine would be fiercely loyal, and I would let it sleep in my bed and sup the blood it needed from my body. Also I would probably send it after Dad's stupid chair, as a favour to the eight-year-old I was. A needle that sharp could do dreadful things to old and soft brown leather. I do not know if this counts as a coherent thought, given its daftness. It is the last thing I remember thinking before I fall asleep, perhaps it was the beginnings of a dream, mixing in the bowl of my poor brain.

Dreams are funny things, though. You need to knead them with the lightest touch possible, too much heat or cold, too full a tummy can lead you down a very scary path.

Legends and their lore inscribed upon them. Complicated simple. All they want's a harbour or a home. The same as anyone.

This is my mother. Laura is my mother. She has two eyes and a nose and a mouth and arms. She likes to laugh, she thinks, but really doesn't. She is the sort of clever where you read books and let other people do things for you. She is quiet in company. She bullies Simon slightly, rests her hand upon his cuff and asks him to do things for her, to drive her places and to buy her things. To put the bottles in the bottle bank on his way home. Her eyebrows are dyed black when she remembers. Eyelashes too. She thinks tattoos are common. If she were to get them, they would be the cosmetic kind. The startled eyebrows underneath your eyebrows. Scarlet line that borders lips so you commit to just one shade of lipstick every day. I think they would be fun to do, even those ones. Imagine if your hand slipped, like. Imagine if ...

I used to always do that in the dentist's. Imagine things. Words to pictures. Pictures into colours. Colours warping into other pictures. My hands can build them better than my tongue.

It's been a year. I used to go quite regularly before. When you have money you don't think about the cost of boring things at all. It's just a thing that's done for you. End of. They met at college, Mam and Dad. She was doing a BA and he was doing Business, but they had friends in common. Back when she had friends.

She has more opinions now than she did before. But she doesn't back them up with any action. I'm the one who takes care of it all. Who keeps receipts in case we can get tax back. Who gets a wrench when the pipe beneath the sink begins to leak. Who replaces fuses. She could do it when it was a thing to placate Dad. She kept it all nice then. But now she doesn't have to do it out of fear, and so we find she can't.

I wonder if I am the same. Because I am afraid of what will happen if I do not keep it all together. Strung along, like crappy paper bunting. Bunting wouldn't be a bad tattoo. With lettering in to celebrate something that was important. You could have it coloured, black and white and falling down with two birds flying off it. A lot of people have tattoos of birds. Because they're pretty. I draw a cat that's eating up a bird with pretty feathers. I draw a ballerina with one leg.

My parents met at college. Isn't that normal? And they fell in love and they got married. That is normal too. They were together for a lot of years and then he met another woman and suddenly they weren't any more. My mother finds it hard. But she's so pretty and she's already met another man, so I reckon it will all be fine. That's the most I've shared with anybody here. Or anyone at all, apart from Anna.

Sheila's parents split up too. She hasn't told us why. Maybe she doesn't know. I don't really want to know or care. She's mad to go out drinking recently. Asking us how she'd get fake ID. If I know anyone who'd buy us drink and we could all go dancing. I think she wants to do all dangerous things so Mam or Dad will scoop her up and mind her. It doesn't work that way, though. Mams and dads are people. And they have to mind themselves as well.

Mam has her work cut out for her there. She told me once when she was drunk in bed that she was sorry. Sorry she had brought me into this. I could take that in several ways, instead I've pinned it to the back of my brain. To revisit later when there's time. I don't know if I love Laura. But I need her. Until I turn eighteen. And even then. Because she bore witness. She saw it too; and, even if she won't always acknowledge it, that's kind of more than other people do. I need to be reminded it was real, because it's here in me. Everything that happened lives inside the meat of me and no matter how I try I cannot scoop it out and she has it too. This thing in you sucks out all the juice and dries life up so you can click by click through days and days until the bedroom door snaps closed behind you and it's finished. It's just with her, the door that stops her normally is the front one.

She used to tell me stories when I was little. About artists and the things they drew. I liked the way the gods played games with mortals. I liked the way she'd tell me about secret things that hid inside big paintings.

'Look for the little dog with the rasher,' she'd say.

Or 'Can you spot who's just about to burst out crying?'

She likes the old stuff, cream and black and full of beards and shadows. Or plates of food.

The kind of stuff I do she thinks is crap. A worrying sort of crap that lets people know how messed up she has made me with her silence and her tolerating Dad. Thing is, though, I mean, we all do it a bit. Sheila wants to go out on the tear. Joanne writes poems about ex-boyfriends that she doesn't have. And they're pretty detailed and things. There are an awful lot of piercings in our school. A lot of anger carved into the desks and scrawled on bathroom doors and etched in lockers.

My drawings are kind of the most average thing about me, really. My brain's the thing that should make her afraid. It's ticking all the time. It's going to blow. And she will have me locked up somewhere safe and go on mini-breaks with Simon and his wallet. Which is fine with me.

Somewhere safe sounds lovely, as it happens. Safety is appealing. I draw a room with three white walls and tiles upon the floor. A black stick/shadow crouches on the floor and shaves its legs and hums.

I draw four-letter words to write on knuckles: LOVE and HATE and KISS and KILL and PRAY and BLOW and SOFT and HARD and SHHH and TICK and TOCK and TICK and BOOM and NEAT and TIDY. SOFA, SIGN and CALM and RUIN and RAGE.

A PICTURE THAT YOU LOVE
AND MADE YOU BLEED

First the sailors caught it from their travels. Then the ladies caught it from the men.

Mother wakes me up at eight o'clock. She has to work and I have to go to school, she says, as well. I cough and cough and tell her I feel rotten, this is not a lie.

She sighs and tells me to 'Go to the doctor so, if you feel rotten.'

I ask her for some money for the doctor.

'Use your own, if you really feel that bad,' she says, all smug like she's won something.

I turn my back on her and fall asleep.

In the olden days, there were some ladies. Being full of pictures was their job. All you needed for it was a body. A body and a story and tattoos.

Our doctor's surgery is between 9.30 and 11.30. You have to make an appointment if you want to go after that. But when I ring for an appointment, there isn't one. I sleep till ten, then dress and head to where his office is. It's not much of a journey, thirty minutes walking. It feels like for ever, though. I want to faint. I keep having to lean on things. Walls and lamp-posts and so on. My throat is very sore and I can't breathe through my nose, so when I breathe the cold air in my mouth it stings like lemon juice upon a wound.

Lemon juice is a natural antiseptic. Mam tried it on me once when she didn't have any Dettol under the sink. I had a cut on my forehead from falling in the playground. It dripped right down my skin and into my eye. My tear duct burned, it was the worst pain ever I had felt. Up till then, anyway.

I was kidnapped by savages, you would say, with halting candour. My father held me down while they looked on. They forced him, though, he didn't want to do it. He had to, though. They would have had me killed.

I feel very sorry for myself. I'm supposed to work the late shift tonight. I message Rob to swap shifts. He is always looking for hours, because he never has enough money for the things he wants. If he got a tattoo it would be a snake curled around a wizard's staff that blossomed flowers. Small, though. He wouldn't like anything too big.

He pierced a hundred pictures on my body. Beads of sweat and little beads of blood. Tracing first, then stabbing in the colour. Until I was a canvas not a girl.

I plan that in my big fat bricky head until I reach the doctor's. The waiting room is full of foreign babies. I know that they are foreign because their parents are murmuring words of comfort to their children, all in different tongues. Baby after baby sees the doctor. I am drifting into sleep when they call my name.

You would remove your shawl and stretch your arms. They'd circle you. Your nape, your shoulder blades. The soft curve of your waist beneath a corset. Your normal shade peeks through like holes in lace.

The doctor has a nice office. The chairs are comfy here and there are lots of comforting certificates on the walls. He is a nice man, and I know I shouldn't but I find my throat constricting as he closes the door behind us. He is wearing an embroidered waistcoat, like something a badger in a children's book would wear. Not just that, though. Because that would be creepy.

All lies of course, the savages had better things to do. But proper ladies don't choose things like this. They certainly don't choose their illustrations. A bible verse for piety. A virtue. Picture of a saint. A floral thing.

He says I have a head cold and chronic fatigue and tells me to get myself to bed. He writes me a note for the rest of the week, which is lovely. He asks me if Mam is waiting outside. I say she is, because I don't want him to worry. I am a little worried myself, though. I don't know if I can make it home without fainting.

You want to show that you're a lovely person. That you are good, though they can see your ankles, thighs and arms. You're not a harlot, though you wanted this.

I stop in a pharmacy and buy some cold and flu remedies. I get hot water at a deli counter. It is not very clean and the guy behind it is not wearing gloves. What a rebel! Their ham slicer is the same as our ham slicer, and I give him a knowing look, which he interprets as flirting, as opposed to a collegial acknowledgement of tools. He winks at me as he hands me the hot drink. I sashay out, wiggling my bottom and stealing most of the napkins from the counter.

I am always surprised when people look at me as if

they want me, surprised and scared. I know that I'm a girl and girls are supposed to be all pretty and so on but sometimes I wake up and decide to try not to be: baggy clothes that hide my figure, hair any old way I please, face unwashed and no mascara or anything. Other times I try my very best. My best is not like everybody's best. I mean, I'm not deformed or anything else. Sometimes I feel as though I am, as though my life is tattooed on my face in thick black gothic font. No-one likes a victim. Everyone feels sorry for her, though.

They'd pay to gawp a little at your body. They'd look you up and down. You would remove your clothes. That's part of it. A most important part. They need to see it all. Examine every picture, every mark. Take their time.

On the walk home I constantly blow my nose. Loads of stuff comes out: none of it delightful. I am bundled up like a baby in jumpers and coats, two scarves, a hat and gloves. I'm still cold, though. Even though I'm sweating I am cold. I feel like I am melting from the inside, that bits of me are falling out and won't grow back. I plug my Walkman into my ears and listen to the dulcet tones of the radio. People phoning in to complain about things.

There's something magical about a picture etched upon

some skin. There's something magical about a woman showing you her body. Worth the ticket price and worth the wait.

They are complaining about teenagers and the things that they get up to. One woman's girl refuses to wear panties. This is not a normal thing, though. The woman would probably like for it to be a trend, a sign that we are all growing progressively sluttier, but the girl is probably acting out, or trying to impress some boy who doesn't give a toss about her. She is fourteen.

Your pain is magic too, it makes you innocent and not complicit. A victim, not a person. Did it hurt they wonder. Did they hold her down and did she scream. Some of them might ask and you will lie to them. It was not the way you say it was. It didn't happen that way.

When I was fourteen I was being raped. I am sixteen now and he is not the last person that I slept with. I sleep with Tom and every time I do I feel like I am cleaning myself out, choosing for myself instead of being chosen. Maybe the woman should look long and hard at her own home life before she starts to ring presenters looking for an easy way to solve her daughter flashing her vagina.

It was simpler. It was more complex. And you said yes.

You welcomed what they drew. You needed money and you needed love and you were never beautiful before and now you are.

The first time that I slept with Tom, I cried and cried and cried right after. He did not know what was going on at all, the poor fellow. It wasn't about him. I think it was because it wasn't a big deal. It always seems to be for other girls. But I was used to it by then, you see. I'd done it so, so often.

A lovely girl.
A titillating freak.

The girls I go to school with have a different view of things than I do and sometimes I hate them for it because I deserved to have the same and still I couldn't. Not that I think my innocence is located in my girl parts or anything. I went to counselling once, but Mam doesn't like me going because she thinks that the counsellor will say it's all her fault that Dad did what he did to me and then I'll leave and Mam will be left with no-one.

The word tattoo *can also mean a rhythm beaten with something on something else. A verb. A noun. A drumming with a hand on a table, a spoon on a juice box. There is a rhythm to the process of tattooing; the needle vibrates up and down, up and down, in and out, out and in and out. The ink must be indelible.*

Tom is my counsellor, in a way. Not that I tell him stuff, but when he's around me I feel normal. And I almost feel like I could tell him sometimes. He knows it wasn't my first time. When we did it. It was his, but it wasn't mine. Or maybe it was in a way. Not physically, but I mean, it was the first time I had made the choice. Away from all the stuff that had gone on, I felt empowered.

I'm on the pill but sometimes I forget. We don't use condoms. I can't bear them. I used to leave them around, hoping Mam would find them. And when she did, she threw them on the fire and told me not to be so disgusting. This was when I was only young. I couldn't say the words yet, couldn't tell her. I wanted her to look at me and know.

The word tattoo came out of Polynesia. According to the Internet at least.

People can't do that in real life, though. Unless they want to find out, I mean. That sort of looking's different from the usual. Harder. More intense. Also, she had her own stuff going on. I mean, I heard things. After a while, Dad didn't bother hiding what he was. From me, I mean; he hid it from my mother. She still said 'not in front of the child', but it was like a line from a script, recited out of habit.

In Japan, they call them irezumi. *It means to put ink in. Insert it, like. Tattooing in Japan is very old. They did it before Christ was born in Bethlehem and time restarted, like in science fiction. I wonder did he ever get tattoos? The Bible doesn't like them, I think. Piercings too. And shellfish. And gay people. Swathes of things dismissed because: The Lord. In Japan, they put the gods on bodies. The Shinto ones. The shining woman's nice. She has all rays and things.*

Dad once said to me in all earnest, 'I would never raise my hand to a woman.' We were watching a film about some lady spy, who got punched in the face a lot. I told Mam that the next day and we both nearly wet ourselves laughing, doing his voice and saying it over and over again. I remember we were in the kitchen and he was at work. I must have been off sick that day as well, because I wasn't at school. Maybe it was holidays. Anyway, it felt great to be laughing at Dad. A bold kind of great. I think that was the beginning of it being talked about. The stuff.

Before, Mam and me kind of used to pretend that it didn't happen. Because we couldn't pretend that it was normal, you see. We'd see normal on the telly and in books and so we knew what it looked like. I saw it at the houses of my friends as well, when I went to visit them. But we could be normal too when there were people over. When I was a kid I thought that all daddies hit all mammies when they were annoyed. I don't remember when I copped on to the fact that they did not. Did I tell someone about it and get told that it did not happen in their house? I wish I could remember. When I was small is very hazy, it feels like a box of photographs and ticket stubs. There's loads of blanks and not much filling in. Some bits are really sharp and clear, but for other things I need more information. There's no point dwelling, though. You can't undo the things that have been done.

For centuries, they chiselled and they gouged and they used wood. And Nara Ink besides. Nara Ink is black outside the body. Under skin it turns to bluest-green. You train and train to learn the old ways now. You need to find a master who will teach you. And it takes years and years to learn the craft.

I don't like that Mam takes his money. Wants it, like. Actively demands sometimes. She calls him asking. He transfers it. She hasn't given him our address yet. I do not want her to. I know he's asked. I know that we need it and he deserves to have to pay for what he's done. But there's something about it that makes me feel like he is compensating us for what he did. Like, when he gave me my pocket money on Fridays, when we all still lived together, I would put it in a drawer and look at it and feel like he was paying me for sex. Like I had become his whore with the simple act of accepting ten euro or whatever he felt like parting with that week.

My brain hurts from all these memories. I try my best to make them go away most of the time but when I let them in it's like a flood and I can't help but feel all the resentful self-indulgent feelings that I'm well aware do me no good at all.

My pillow smells like dried spit, but as I kick off my shoes and cuddle between the sheets, it feels like comfort. Mam has left a list of things for me to do. I am not going to do them, though. She can do them. It's not like I'm on holidays or something. It's not like I suddenly have loads of free time to hoover and bleach toilets and make lasagnes to freeze. I am sick. I think that I deserve to be sick for just one day.

Irezumi are a clue that someone works for the yakuza. Scary people, them. Or so I've heard from Hollywood and things. But other people have them too. Warriors, Kabuki masks, heroes, carp and dragons.

These are things my mother says and means:
'I love you.'

'I hate her.' About Breda.

'I wish things were more simple.'

'He was bad for us. We're better off.'

'You need to help out more.'

'I can't handle this at all.'

'Where is/are my bag, purse, mobile, keys?'

'How was school?' She wants me to say 'fine'.

'Sure, you'll be grand. You're young. You're not like me.'

'I wish …' And then she wishes.

'School is more important than this job.'

'Shut your trap.'

'Can you lend me a fifty till the weekend?' And when I do she never gives it back. We both know that she won't but she pretends and so do I.

'Simon's coming over.' This means tidy up.

You don't have to be criminal to find the lore behind all that appealing. But probably you should be. To make the meaning stronger as it's etched.

I'll do it all tomorrow. I promise. I have the radio on still. I like to fall asleep listening to something, not being alone in the room. In the dark. It isn't dark, though; it is bright outside. My curtains are practically useless, the light shines through them almost more brightly than it does through glass. My head aches and a drowsy numbness pains my sense as though of vodka I had drunk. That's Keats, except the vodka bit. I do try to learn things. Sometimes some of it does stick. Keats died young. I wonder if it was a snotty death. That would have been undignified. If I die, I'd like to turn into ash like vampires on telly, just *pouff!!* and I'd be gone. No bodily fluids, no disgusting cleaning up to do. Just once over the carpet with the vacuum cleaner and then once more, just to be sure. Empty the hoover bag and that's me done. I don't want to be buried or burned or anything. I just want to be gone.

You see tattoos on warriors a lot. To intimidate their foes. On warriors. Of warriors. There's something about tolerating pain that implies strength. I disagree. It doesn't mean you're strong. It means you've hurt. Which doesn't make you special, but it's pretty.

My sheets have a boy-band on them from the nineties. They are called The Backstreet Boys and have really clean and shiny faces. It is supposed to be ironic. I bought them in a charity shop. They are my new guild of dolls, the only boys I'll have inside my bedroom. Tom has visited here, but not upstairs. Not inside my bed. I pretend that it is a practical consideration – it is smaller than his bed, and there are privacy issues, with Mam being around the odd time. I like to keep my room all to myself. No boys allowed and certainly no men.

I didn't want to bring my sheets from home. When you buy things second-hand, you must be very careful, because they can harbour bedbugs, scabies, crabs and other body lice. You never know who has used them before you. Tapes, I think, are fine. I mean, it's not like I am going to eat them. Clothes, sheets, curtains and so on are a different matter altogether. You have to soak them in disinfectant and then wash them in the washing machine on the proper setting. Really hot for towels and sheets, but not for things that say hand-wash or dry-clean only. We did bring some things from the old house, the one we lived in before. The spare TV, some towels and shelves and things. The couch. I don't like looking at the stuff that we had there. I know that it would be very stupid to leave all of it to him, but it reminds me of the way things were and I don't like it.

Mam wanted the computer, but he wouldn't give it to her, even though he already has a laptop. I'd like to get one if we ever have the money. A second-hand one would be less than two hundred, I think. If you got a deal. We could do it, if we put aside a tenner a week for twenty weeks. We won't, though. It always seems to go on other things. I often think about the things I'd buy, if only I had saved sufficient tenners. Phones and laptops, MP3 players, artificial skin and needles. Loads of ink.

The Celts did it too, back in the day. I imagine them with wild, woad-coloured markings. Not crosses yet. Before. Beasts and torcs and fat, angry-looking things woven intricate, the one atop the other. Swords. Spears. Cauldrons. Stones. Leaves and trees and bands of gold and silver.

I fall asleep and, for once, I do not have a dream. Just nothing. It's so nice.

Tom rings three times. He really wants to see me. I tell him I am sick, but he says, 'Today, it has to be today.' That's not like him. I wonder if he is all right, but I can't stomach leaving the house, not again. I tell him if he wants to talk to me, he can tell me what he needs to on the phone. I am too sick to be around him. When I am around him, I want to look pretty and it takes too much effort to look pretty when my head feels like a bag of painful goo. I am not in the mood to be looked at or touched. I want to be all by myself and sit on the couch and watch bad television. I pull my thin duvet down the stairs after me, like a child with a blankie.

I didn't have a blankie as a child. Some of my friends did; they'd huff it like it was paint or glue and suck their fingers. The guild of dolls were what I had, and they were not always friendly. I was constantly trying to please them.

Once Christians came, illuminated manuscripts were just

as intricate. I saw the Book of Kells once, with my school. Vellum, our teacher said, was made out of the skin of baby cows. We are mammals too. How much would someone sacrifice for art? I wonder did the monks ever use their own skin. I know that they used to flay themselves in penance. It is only a small step to the next thing. What better use of skin? How deep does someone cut to make a parchment, how soon until it grows back again or will it ever?

Mam spent a long time in the hospital, and Dad had to get me ready for school and all that sort of thing. I suppose that was the beginning of it. All those baths and things. It's strange that I could have a brother now. He'd be almost ten. Mam said that he was whole when he came out. He could have survived if it had been a normal labour, but she was pretty banged up as well. From her fall. There was a lot of blood and chunks of stuff. Dad didn't get it all. I found some behind the toilet. He was never very good at cleaning up, but if Mam missed out on something he would notice right away. Mam was very sad for a long time after they took all the poison out of her blood. She hadn't been sure that she wanted to bring another child into this house, and she had said as much to Dad when they were rowing. So that made it kind of all her fault that the baby died inside her belly.

I brought her nightie into bed with me while she was

gone. I had a pain in my tummy whenever I thought about her and the baby that had died. He wasn't allowed to be buried in the graveyard. I don't know what they did with his little body. I never got to see it. Mam says that it was smaller than any other baby. Smaller than anything. But it had hair, a full head of see-through hair like she does. My hair is the same colour as Dad's. The kind of blond that is almost red. People always say that it is pretty, but I don't care much for it.

There is something in us that makes us want to draw on ourselves, on other people. Talismans, identifying marks.

There is a teddy-bear on *The Antiques Roadshow* that is worth two thousand pounds. It has a very grumpy little face and it looks stiff, like it would hurt to cuddle it. I love the idea of finding something in the attic that was worth a lot, some sort of treasure. Hidden things. Enough for me to study for a while. Or even give up work in my exam years. That would be magical. It would never occur to me to take anything to be valued, though. I mean, you don't do that in the normal course of things, do you? Well, some people might, but is it free? And do they take a cut? I would probably know all these things if I was from the kind of family that grew treasures in their attic. I would also be a magnificent horsewoman and a keen gardener. And know instinctively what spoon to use and how to address titled people. Basically, I would be an English person. Irish people's attics are crap. They are full of weapons and potatoes, and not even good potatoes, like Kerr's pinks, or good weapons, like shiny swords or valuable antique guns. It is all pointy sticks and pikes. A pike is a pointy stick with a blade on the top. I imagine it was quite a moment, when it was invented. Lots of champagne and self-congratulation all around.

I wish I had a secretly expensive teddy-bear. And proper tissues, the ones that come in boxes instead of stupid loo-roll that Mam steals from the museum. It is in ridiculously big rolls and does not fit on a toilet-roll holder. She was at me to bring some home from school as well, but I did not like that idea even a little bit. Silly Mam, she has always loved free stuff. She always takes loads of sugar packets from restaurants, even though neither of us takes sugar in our tea at all. We have a drawer full of them, also plastic forks and knives and spoons. The heavy-duty kind. She uses them to clean things like the little gap between the floor and the shower tray that gets black in it, or so she says. I have never once seen her clean the little gap between the floor and the shower tray that gets black in it. She docs, however, occasionally muster up the energy to stand over me when I clean the house, including the little gap between the floor and the shower tray that gets black in it, so she can tell me where I'm going wrong. I am going wrong in a lot of places.

Dad used to do that too, but not to me, to her. And he wouldn't really give advice, just wait for her to make a mistake and then get cross with her. He was a bit like a crueller version of the Dog Whisperer. Except that Mam was a woman and not a dog and the Dog Whisperer would never beat the shit out of a dog and systematically abuse the child that the dog bore him. He seems like a good guy, the Dog Whisperer. He has 'kind eyes'. Although you cannot tell from people's eyes, not really. Somebody once said that to my dad, at a Christmas party in our house. I think it was the woman from work that he ended up having the affair with. He was a really shit father on many levels, now that I come to think of it.

They're living together, my father and that woman. Breda. She wears big necklaces and has a wide, fat smile. She is 'a laugh', 'a breath of fresh air'. Thirty-five. The reason he left us or she left him. I can't decide which one. Sometimes she says it was because of the abuse, but really I'm not sure. She put up with all that for years and years and suddenly there's Breda and confronting. We aren't taking him to court or whatever, because it would be expensive and also Mam is scared of what he'd do if we dragged all the private things into the open. We tried before, around the time we left. It didn't go so well. We don't speak with my dad's side of the family. And they don't speak to us. And that is fine. I kind of miss my gran, though. I look like her. I kind of thought she loved me.

You can use ink to protect yourself from bad spirits. Bad spirits are everywhere – look outside the window. If you do not like everything you see, the thing you do not like is probably a bad spirit, or the fault of a bad spirit.

The other woman thinks that Mam's a liar. Mam is a liar, but not about that. She lies about other things. Like money and how safe we are. We really are not safe. Also, sometimes I think that she resents me, I can see it in her eyes, so sometimes when she says she loves me I think she lies about that. She lies to Simon too. I mean, she kind of has to. I don't think he has the least idea about all the baggage the both of us have. She lies about how much she drinks as well. Sometimes she forgets to eat, but she needs a drink to go to sleep. Not that I blame her or anything. It is kind of understandable. But when she pretends to be this caring, good mother who is also functional she is fooling no-one. Well, she is kind of fooling everyone. Just not me. I am on to her.

She has not made me a dinner in about a month and a half. That is not maternal. My friends get dinners every single day.

I am not hungry for dinner today, though, I am too sick. I wanted a piece of toast earlier, but the bread has gone off. Like, seriously gone off, blossoming with green and bluish mould. I hate that kind of thing. When our food is not fit to be eaten it makes me feel really slovenly or something. Like I'm not doing as good a job of living without Dad. Like we needed him in some way. Which I suppose we kind of may have done. Financially and for the routine. But obviously we are better off without him. I just wish he was worse off without us. He isn't. He has his girlfriend, they live in our old house, he's kept his job and nobody knows why we left, I think they all presume it was because of the new girlfriend. Which does make sense – I mean, a lot of people leave their wives and most of them aren't evil. Some of them are, I assume.

I'd love to see him go to prison for what he did to me. To Mam as well, but that is up to her. She seems quite OK with shutting up. With letting things roll on.

Evils, pain, vulnerability in life or battle – a little ink can remedy these things. Goddesses and gods upon your back or thighs to guide and watch over you. Protective ones. The old kind, that only really live on Wikipedia.

Around five, when she is due to come home from work, I tidy everything up and head to bed, as neat as a hotel, the couch and coffee table in my wake. I turn off the little red light on the TV, not just with the remote. If she could see that I'd been up already then she would want me to have done all the things on her list of jobs. She likes to come home to a clean house, Mam does. I wish this extended to actual cleaning. She is like Dad in that way, actually. Although she wouldn't welcome that comparison. No-one would, to Dad, not if they knew him. I think that would be the worst thing I could say to her. And I could say a lot.

Curl up under duvet. Sniff the pillow like it was my friend.

In my room there are some other treasures. The last few remnants of the guild of dolls. Pink Doll, Red-dog Doll and Black Doll, who has Blue Doll's arm sewn on to her. Black Doll was once my mam's, she is a golliwog with big white eyes and a wide red mouth. She has the stiffest stuffed legs and the softest stuffed belly. Her hair is short black wool and she does not belong inside the world. You wouldn't find a doll like her in toy-shops now. She was always gentler with me, Black Doll. Maybe because she is an ugly thing, an ugly kind of pretty, I like her contrasting colours a whole lot. Maybe I will draw her on my body when I'm older and she would sleep with me every night to comfort me from all the hurts that linger and accuse.

I also have amassed a bag of needles, all in different shapes and sizes. Some are blunt, some sharp as little teeth. You can collect them from different places. Some I harvested from the floor of the home-ec room, others from the road. You get little sewing kits in hotels sometimes. We had to stay in a hotel until we found this place. (That ate into our savings quite a lot.) Any time I saw the maid's unguarded cart, I'd grab a kit or two. They come in handy and it isn't really stealing if it's something that will be free anyway. To other people. I leave my bag of needles in a drawer, but recently I have been considering moving it to my wardrobe hidey-hole. I think I need more secrets in my life. Things all for myself that no-one knows. Good secrets, not bad ones. I do not have the best track record with secrets. Keeping of. Telling of.

I do have a good track record with having colds. I usually get at least one a winter. They come for me – lie in wait inside my throat and brain, all my secret hollows that can pump and swell. Waiting for wet feet to drag through puddles. Cold sleepless nights. A dearth of orange juice consumed. Something I can blame and then they happen. My glands are up. They feel like two tiny Adam's apples that have drifted to the sides for some unknown reason. Boredom or whatever.

Badhbh. Morrigan. Kali. Lillith. Nemain. Isis. Neith.

To draw those on a person would be something. Victoria. Nike, bathed in war. Tanit. Juno. Sekhmet and the Keres. Bastet, Macha, Hypatia, Medeina. So many stories living there. Inked into the dermis of the world. Stories waiting to be turned to pictures. Pictures waiting to be drawn on skin and people waiting for the ones they need.

I do not like the story of the apple. It is all Eve's fault, and I don't think it would be. Not really. If she had been made of something other than a rib then maybe she would not have talked to snakes. She wasn't even made of the full cage, just one sole rib. I bet that she was skinny. Pictures usually show her skinny. She must have been, if all she ate was fruit. If I drew her, she would be angular and long, hard-looking, like a bone. All canals and crests, facets and foveas. Every labyrinth displayed beneath the skin. My Eve would not be sinewed. Lean and snake-like, icy-eyed and proud. Scheming. The kind of temptress who would eschew clothes even after apples had been crunched and knowledge gained.

I am more like my idea of Lilith. I like my clothes and hate my naked body. Its pits and bumps, its hairy bits and smooth. Between my legs is hairy as a beard. Before Tom was there I did not trim, I grew it out to try to hide the lips. The sinful things. It did feel like a sin, what we were doing, me and Dad. I know that it was not a sin for me.

But when he made me do some things I felt somehow complicit. Our secret practices, hidden from my mother and his wife. He'd threaten her sometimes. If I didn't do things. But mostly he did not have to threaten very much at all, it was implied that kicking up a fuss would be a bad idea. Usually I went outside my head and thought of stories, pictures or TV shows that I had only seen the first half of. I'd make up the ending in my head and close my eyes as often as I could and for as long.

It doesn't always have to be elaborate, though that is half the fun. Runes and stars and angels, eyes and circles. Little things to make a person safer. Nautical stars to guide a sailor home. Certain Thai marks claim they can stop bullets. I wouldn't be the one to test that out but what you want's a picture for your story. To choose the things that people put on you.

Lilith was the wife that came before. I don't know what she was made of. The same stuff that Adam was, I think. She is often drawn with snakes and serpents, like a demon. She was not good enough to stay inside the garden, so they kicked her out, and she was with the demons and they slept with her and she bore demon babes. There is a superstition that she sucks the breath from children for some reason. I draw her with long red hair and yellow hissing eyes. Snakes slick up her belly. Another Lilith hides beneath a hood, the shadow of her face a pretty thing, but sad and also deadly. She kills babies, you see. She is a demon. When you lie with demons that is what you ultimately become. Hard and cruel as you were soft before. That story's in the hollows round the eyes. I shade them in with pencil. A Celtic frame with ivy in around her.

I need to get more colours for designs. The ones I have are cheap and don't do light and dark too well at all. Maybe next time Simon gives me money I could buy some more. I am quiet as panthers in my room. I've never heard a panther. Inky-black and sleek, I imagine them silent as the air when they approach. I draw a half-panther half-Lilith demon. Her eyes are cat's, her skin as black as the skin of Black Doll. I draw a cat with feathers instead of fur. Ripply with contempt is my poor kitten. If I died, I would like to come back as a cat, I think. They do not care and they survive in wilderness a-stalk.

A choice you made
and now you have to live with

A teardrop for a murder, three dots on the hand for the Father, Son and Holy Ghost, the eye of Horus to ward off betrayal, five dots show that time was spent in prison — you are the fifth, stuck fast inside the walls.

My treasured things are mostly cheap and small. Stories I've been told, old books of drawings. There aren't any people that I love without reservation. Mam is duty; Dad is good as dead. I wish he really were. My friends at school and Tom are more about survival.

I need Tom to feel clean inside myself. Someone who can touch me and not know. Someone who can want me properly, without it being heavy, forced and wrong. I am free now and with his hands he traces all the free parts of me. I do not have to do things I don't want to.

Mam would kick up a fuss if I quit my job, stopped tidying and cleaning. But she couldn't, in all fairness, do a thing to make me work against my will. I'm too big now to be told what to do. Every part of me belongs to me. If I wanted, I could transcribe a novel on my body. I have that power, I have that strength of will. I don't need him, or anyone.

But, universe, it helps to have a friend. Some day, I could even tell him the whole story, maybe. If he sticks around to hear it. I don't think you could expect anyone to stick around after that kind of reveal, though. Maybe out of guilt. I sometimes find myself almost crying after. I pretend it's the release, but it probably isn't. I wonder if I'll ever be OK with everything, like a normal girl. I hope to be a normal girl some day, not to feel as though there is a stain beneath my skin and in my gut and brain and in my being, all that I am painted over skin on dirt invisible. Flaws deepen with age and removal from the home where I was hurt hasn't seemed to make my brain OK. The cracks will broaden. Look at Mam. I'm failing.

Tattoos can guard you, or the other thing. Tell them who you are and what you do.

Maybe if nothing bad was to happen any more. Maybe if Mam married Simon, gave up her job and went back to a time before she hurt inside as well. I wouldn't like to have a man inside the house again. Not any man, no matter how non-threatening. Simon is non-threatening. There is a softness about him: I do not think that he could hurt a person. He catches flies and spiders, lets them out the window. As if they were not little flies and spiders. As if their tiny lives were that important. Mam has done a good job finding the polar opposite of Dad. I don't know if that is what she was going for, but if I were her that is what I would have tried to go for. No point in making the same mistake twice. She guards him like a dragon with a hoard. They dine together in our house and I am not invited. He stays the night, and I should go somewhere and not come back until it's after bedtime.

Laura separates me from her normal life – her boyfriend and the friends she has made at work. She didn't really have that many friends when I was small. Apparently she did, but when she married Dad a lot of them stopped coming. He did not like them, did not like the way she was around them. They didn't stop it all at once, like make some big decision or anything. Drifted, I suppose. Most of them have families of their own by now. Families take time, and if you sense that you are not wanted in a place you don't like to go back and back again. Mam says she should have made more of an effort, but she wanted to please him and thought if she could solve the problem, balance the equation, he would change. A little less outside friendship on her side to equal a little less angriness on his. Only it didn't and she found herself alone and more afraid. As long as I remember she was afraid. She still is, too. And that's no way to live.

Iconography of self – you draw who you are and people see it. Them that have the legend to your map. The ones you get in prison smudged and blue. Ink from ballpoint pens and sometimes soot. Blue roses grow so dangerous on a chest.

I am frightened of a lot of things: spiders, certain doors and chairs, people in big groups, men, women, school being too hard, my limitations, failure, being wrong and heights. I am not afraid of Dad. I will not give him the satisfaction. He has done his worst. If he was going to kill either of us he would have done it on the day we left.

I read this thing online that said that rape is worse than murder for the victim. When you're dead you do not feel a thing, but when you're raped you have to live with it. I hate that way of thinking. Even though I often want to die, I'm glad to live. My life is not my sex. My virtue doesn't live between my legs. You can't take that – it's mine and it is intrinsic. Even when I feel that things are spoiled and wrong I do not wish that I had been strangled or beaten or stabbed to death. I sometimes wish that I did not exist, but that is not the same. If anyone is going to kill me, I want it to be me. It's my life and I deserve to treat it how I want.

How I want is to grow back to normal. To learn what that is and ape it until I become like everybody else. Not somebody who wears herself like clothes that do not fit. Who looks at people from behind her eyes, deciding what they'd do in their darkest moments. How exactly could you fuck me over's what I wonder when I look at people. Because I know that everybody can, and will, and does.

Criminal tattoos are their own language, like the signals that ladies gave with fans in ballrooms past, flirting and informing. Barbed wire crown around the forehead means you're in for ever, no parole. One cat for a thief, two or more cats indicate a gang. A bird flying means that you long for freedom, but who doesn't?

Families are funny things. You do not choose them, and they can be great, like Mam's sister Pat who lives in Australia and does not know the full story, but still called every night for the first month after the separation. She loves Mam and knows how hard it is to leave your husband. She hasn't met me since I was quite small. She might come to visit in the summer, though – she's thinking about that. Dad's mam, Gran, is great, but just to Dad. She loves him very much and minds him terribly. She did not like my mam and blames her for the rift between Dad and me. I do not know if she's been told the truth. I'm fairly sure she definitely has. I didn't get a birthday card this year. She always sends one. Always did before. Laura said it's her, not me, they're cross with but that isn't true, it's both of us, it's all of it and everything. I do not know if I want her to know. It is a tough one.

The problem for me is this: I want the world to know Dad is a rapist, but I don't want to be the victim. Assigning myself that role just seems somehow like a shot in the foot. What can I do if I present myself as just a victim? If the biggest thing about me is that something terrible was done in childhood nights and sometimes childhood days and childhood mornings? I struggle with it, in my head and heart. And what's a rape? I mean, I was twelve when I had full sex but all that stuff before that wasn't rape. It kind of was. It felt the same. A natural progression.

Spiderwebs and tombstones can symbolise the number of years lost to jail. Churches mean that here's the best place for you. But you are trapped. You might as well be dead.

My gran wears lipstick almost always. Little neat heels and brooches. She has a lot of scarves. She shops in boutiques and goes antiquing. She was married to a country doctor. She goes to mass and gardens even though it's hard on her back. When I was small, she'd make me go out weeding. I kind of liked it. Getting my hands and clothes dirty. Dad would laugh as though it didn't matter.

And then blame Mam when he got home, decided that it did matter and found a reason.

Gran is together. Elegant and calm. She does things properly. If she has dinner, there are place settings and courses. If she has scones, a little pot of cream. She heats the milk before she serves you coffee. She likes to read as well, but when she's finished with a book she gives it to a charity shop that day. Unless she'll read it twice. She's very exacting. Has standards, like. Grandad used to say about her 'She'd buy and sell us all' or 'She could do anything at all, that woman.'

She's active in Neighbourhood Watch and she has hobbies and she always votes. She loves her sons. She doesn't talk to me. Maybe she doesn't have our address. But if she wanted it, she'd find a way to get it. If Mam was her, if she was my mam instead of Mam, we would be fine. We'd manage, like. I miss having my gran. I miss having a family that wasn't just my mam and Aunty Pat, who doesn't really count because she's far away. 'Moral support' Mam calls that, which is great for her, but not for me. She sent me a pair of Uggs, when they broke up, and a card about tough times and getting through them. They were a size too big, and let in water.

Dagger means a sex offender. On your face means you're not getting out, you're here forever. Eyelids means you're tough. They use a spoon shoved under not to blind you.

At school I do not want people to know.

At work I do not want people to know.

In the street I do not want people to know.

At home I do, though, when I need to cry and talk and scream because it's real. I have to ask, Why me, why did this happen? I have to moan so I can try to cope. At home there's only Mam, you see, and that's the problem. Because she has enough on her plate, without me adding to it extra crazy. Extra pain.

I'm terrified that she will kill herself. And what would happen then? I would go into care and that would be much worse than now. I wouldn't have a room of my own and barely anybody fosters teens – they prefer little kids with apple cheeks that complement their problems. And how would I feel in a stranger's home with a strange man who'd eye me up and down like a belonging? I need two years before I am a grown-up, but I also need a mam. The one I have is breaking and I'm afraid that all the things I do to keep her from breaking even more, to Sellotape the cracks in her together, aren't working. Also, I feel I am breaking too. Mincing like meat a little day by day. Turning handle grinds me down to grains of human flesh.

Religious things, Madonna and the little Baby Jesus, mean you're loyal. And Catholic, of course. You won't betray your friends to the police. That matters, to a gang. It's good to know.

Soft, soft sleep takes thoughts away from me. I sleep like Beauty if she was no beauty. But all around me things are going on and moving forward. The belt shifts round, towards the register, but I'm not there, I'm just beside it watching from a point that's fixed and I don't want to move but think I should. The tissues on my floor are snotted snow. Steps up stairs and then the door is cracked. The light-bulb in the hall will soon need changing. Mam brings me a honey-and-lemon drink in a cup. It burns my tongue but warms my shivered hands. There isn't whiskey in it and I'm glad. My open tummy couldn't take the weight.

There aren't really any gangs in Ireland, though. Not the kind you draw on with machines. No Crips. No Bloods. No DDP. No Latin Kings. No bratva, triad, mafia, whatever. Our gangsters aren't very picturesque.

The night tonight is like night from a picture. The sky is dark blue and the lights of town are just as good as stars. You cannot see the real stars here, hardly ever. A cold clear night where we used to live was pretty. The sky a dark bowl, filled with tiny holes that let in light. What makes a gang of stars a constellation? A pattern with a name. The names can change as well, the Plough can be a Dipper in the States. The leg of a big bear.

I never joined the dots to see the bear, I can't quite picture it. I like the image, though. A big bear in the sky who looks down on us with kindly bearish eyes. I would like if God was a big bear. It would explain a lot, because bears do not trouble themselves with petty human matters. War, famine, disease are of no concern to bears. The ice-caps melting are a problem. Fewer seals to kill, and hungry bears are angrier and sadder.

My bear up in the sky would roar and rumble, causing storms in all his lonely space. Souls would tremble. Arguments erupt. Hearts harden, soften with his mighty breath.

I draw in my brain the face of the Great Bear. White, brown, wide and almost cartoon-like, with eyes that are innocent and wise at the same time. Everybear and nobear. Bears are not as kindly as we paint them. They can be dangerous things and if you happen upon one in the forest it is inadvisable to greet it like a friend.

Why do we say 'I can't bear it' when things become difficult to tolerate?

Bears are solitary things, so the big bear in the sky would not be lonely. By himself, he would not be afraid.

Our world is one of mythic tales and deeds inside my brain, but outside things are dying. The world the colour ash beside the sky. False light filters through the streets, illuminating dirt. I feel it freezing.

Indelible identifying marks

Placement's as important as the subject. Will it fit and how will it look there? The body has a lot of holes and dents and crevices and curves. You want to find the place that fits the best. If it's a secret. If you want to flaunt it. If it brands you. If it makes you proud.

The sun is bright, even at night. The moon just reflects it on us all. I sometimes feel that sunlight is like the UV light in bathrooms, that it shows the creepy human stains that mar us all, but me more than most people. I have days where the sunlight feels disgusting on my skin. Inching up my arms towards the bits of me beneath my clothes. There is UV ink that you can get, to write on you in secret and people only see it when there is the proper light. Black light. I like that, it's like grown-up Magic Markers, where you would write a note to your friend in the white one and they would colour it in and then read what it said. My favourite was always the black and pink one – I like those two together. They kind of fit.

I have a dress that used to be my mam's which is those colours. It is zebra print, with black collar and cuffs. It is the kind of dress a lady would wear with little gloves. I really like it. When I wear it I feel like I knew Mam before I met her. When she was fun and wore a pretty dress. She can't even remember why she kept it, or maybe she can but isn't telling me. I wore it when Tom took me to the cinema for the first time.

We rarely go anywhere, me and Tom. We stay in. But that is probably because I'm busy. I'd like to think that we would do things if I had more time. Maybe have a proper sort of relationship thing. I'd like to try one out. I do not always want to be alone. Only, like, almost always.

Family's important to almost everyone. A lot of people get their people's names or portraits. Babies' faces grim on hairy calves. It's hard to get the innocence of babies. There's always something older in the eyes.

There are days where I hate all the people in the whole wide world. Teeming like ants, they bustle and they hurt. But I don't want to be alone for ever, I want to make a family of my own, one where no-one is horrible to anyone. I do not mean have kids. I am glad that I didn't ever get pregnant or anything. It was pretty much luck. He didn't always use condoms.

Also, I didn't get my period until after we left – maybe my body was waiting until I was safe. Everyone else had theirs. Not that I did a survey. It seemed like it, though – I kept getting asked for tampons or pads when I was in the bathroom. As if I was a shop. There's nothing to be proud of really, is there? Even though people are. Of growing up. All the little markers. The first times, meaning nothing once they're over. When the mysteries are solved, there's really very little left to do.

Menstruating women are dirty things in lots of cultures. You shouldn't sit where they sit, lie with them or let them pray. The Great Bear in the sky must be perplexed. His eyes have seen so much, you see, so many hurts that make the bear growl softly. So many people and so many lives. I wonder do the stars ever try to count the lives like we count them? They'd have a time because we all keep breeding. So many babies everywhere. I do not like to look at little girls. I always wonder what their lives are like once they go home, because people can look happy and be sad.

People can even *be* happy and have a hellish life apart from that. Just because something rotten happened to you, or happens every day, does not mean constant gloom. People seem to think it does. Joanne was reading this article about a girl like me and said, 'Her life is ruined for ever now,' and it isn't, but Jesus that was jarring.

I asked her if she really meant for ever.

'Yeah,' said Sheila. 'She could get, like, counselling. Or something …' Her voice trailed off, she didn't sound convinced.

'Counselling doesn't solve *anything*,' said Joanne. 'And even if it did, it would take years. How are you supposed to deal with stuff like that and have a normal life?'

I asked her what was in her sandwich then. Chicken, pesto, rocket. Sounded nice.

I don't get why people tell their stories in magazines. I mean, I'd like to tell Dad's story, but not mine. Put up posters: 'Have you seen this man? He is a rapist and he does disgraceful things to women. He answers to the name of Francis, and is often seen in suits. When not in suits, he wears rugby shirts tucked into jeans. Mutton dressed as somewhat younger mutton. I would like another father, please.'

But when it comes to putting it into words. Saying this is a thing that happened to me and it was bad and look at me and know, I just don't see the point. What would it accomplish? Nothing would get easier or better. The people who know about it don't care. And the people who don't know about it wouldn't know how to deal with me any more if I was suddenly a broken thing out loud.

Babies trump flags though, in my opinion. You could do a foetus shape on someone's wrist or a cartoonish little illustration. A flag is just a flag and flags can stand for creepy things quite easily. Get out of here. This is my flag. My land.

I'd make an offering if I'd an altar. Maybe I could build one in my room. Put food on it, my skeleton and drawings. A bit of the machine. Some honey and some sweets for gods or ghosts. I wish my bear were real enough for me to be a supplicant. I would confess my sins, he wouldn't care and I would stroke his fur amongst the stars, the weather cold as needles but his body warm enough to keep me quick and breathing in the darkness. Please, Great Bear, take back my life and let me live a new one. One where my father is a different man, a famous tattoo artist and we live in Amsterdam or somewhere warm and I am his apprentice and Mam is happy all the live-long day.

I'd settle for not being for ever ruined, Great Bear, but if you don't ask you don't get is what they say, so thought I might just ask for something I'd enjoy. More money or fewer problems would be fine, though. More of a fighting chance. And would that be OK?

Joanne told me the name for the almost invisible line of hair that goes down to your groin. The treasure trail. It is more visible on men, and does not always lead to any treasure.

Bit misleading. I would prefer my trail to lead to cake. The things I draw for there: A slice of cake. A dragon guarding something. Enter at your own risk in gothic font.

I'd live my whole life backwards all again if I could just unlive it, have it all unhappen to me and feel right, inside myself, and not be ruined. That was what a woman was, in olden times, if she was touched by a man before her marriage, ruined. Not that things are that bad for us now, but it is so taboo what I've been through that I kind of feel I am. I mean, who'd have me? There is so much hatred and resentment in my gut. I am so angry, a nasty little beast filled up with woes and bitterness.

I suppose all words were once unknown to me, I found it hard to shape some of them in my awkward mouth, even after I was speaking up. Incest was one in particular. I hated it. Hate it still, it sounds quite like a period of time, a break, a rest. Of course I know that it means something else. Of course.

My father's mother, Gran, says that the worst thing that a woman can be is sour. Which is rich coming from pursed-up, moaning her. She judges everyone, and the only ones who pass are the people that came out between her legs. No matter how flawed they are. She liked me when I was younger, I think. It is easy to like babies, though, and children. When I got big and awkward, she was still quite fond of me, her favourite but less cuddly and so on. Since I left and went to live away from Dad with Mam, she doesn't come to see me or anything. I rang her on her birthday, but she doesn't like to talk on telephones – they make her feel uncomfortable for some reason I do not understand.

My favourite memory of Gran involves her knitting and telling me a story, which was the plot of one of her favourite films, *Seven Brides for Seven Brothers*. Her version was more savage than the movie, though. She went into lurid detail about how scared the six kidnapped girls were, and in her tale they had to go through horrible hardships, rats in walls and very little food. They had to get married, in my gran's story. But even though it was an awful tale, I felt so safe and fascinated sitting on her lap, as the needles clicked and her mouth moved squishily around.

She wasn't great at storytelling, Gran. Most of her tales were versions of a movie she had seen. 'The pictures' she called them. I like pictures too, but different kinds. Gran was great at violence. Always threw in lots of lovely peril. And her fingers worked. She's never perfectly still, for all her poise. She has to be doing something. Fair Isle's what she liked, intarsia as well. Weaving pictures on a woollen canvas line by line. Sometimes she wouldn't tell me what they were for ages, make me guess and guess and it was fun.

I must have been quite young, because she got bad arthritis in her hands years ago and had to give up knitting. I would hate to give up working with my hands. It is one of the only things that I am good at. If I couldn't draw, or work my machine I don't know what I'd do. It would unhinge me more than I'm unhinged.

Flash means pre-made stencils. It would be more interesting to design your own, but pre-made ones take up a lot less time. These are the ones you look at in the binder on the walls.

Giving people identifying marks would save a lot of time, if only you could choose the marks for them. Warning signs on problematic men, with different colours for the level of inadvisability involved. Low levels would be for people who like a drink a bit too much and occasionally make off-colour jokes in loud voices. Little things like that. Dad would be the worst level, possibly bright red with skulls around. I do not know if that would put folk off, though. People seems to like a bit of danger.

Anna from my old school's boyfriend gave her different drugs, out of his mother's medicine cabinet, just to see what would happen to her, like some sort of wicked scientist. He usually takes them himself too. Painkillers, really strong ones for her back, are the nicest. The anti-depressants don't do much at all, so Anna says. She thought she would have been tripping all over the place because they are supposed to be for head-stuff. Anna's wild like that. She likes to do the things that break your brain. Drinking till you vomit, pills. She had a box inside her school bag with about seventy painkillers in it. She said it was for her period. She'd pop about twelve a day. I'd give out and she'd tell me the recommended dosage was a 'serving suggestion' and she'd built up a tolerance with time.

I haven't thought of Anna in a long time. She emails me but I don't reply for ages. Sometimes, though, I write to her to see how my old school is doing without me. Things are just the same, from what she says. The only one who misses me is Anna. I wonder how long it will take for her to stop. We were close because we were both on the edge of the group. Invited to the big things, but not let in on any secrets first. Both quiet, both pale, both a bit reserved. Anna was the first person I thought that I could tell outside the family. I didn't tell her all of it, but some. The hitting stuff.

She's the only proper friend I have. I'm still deciding whether I should cut her out or keep her. It changes from day to day. Anna is angry that Dad is not in prison. I explained why Mam thought it would be better if we didn't take that path. She thinks it is the only path to take. She hasn't said anything to anyone, but maybe she has. You cannot really trust people too much, it isn't that the two of us were super-super close. Except we might have been a bit. I find it hard to know what friendship is, because there are the people you hang out with and then there are the ones that would actually miss you if you died. The ones you matter to, or whatever. Anna was my that.

Not that I was all confidey in her, I'm not all that confidey. We were at her house, her parents were out and we were drunk. She tried to kiss me on the mouth for some stupid reason. It was like really important to her that she kiss me on the mouth and I didn't want her to and I pushed her away and started crying and she thought it was because I didn't like her any more and she was all upset and I said Dad once tried to kiss me just like that, just to see how it sounded coming out. We were already leaving him by then. Mam knew about Breda and it felt less like a smashing to reveal, the cracks already there and me just widening them with a fingernail.

Anna freaked right out and said, *That's weird. That's weird. That's weird. That's weird.* Over and over again she called it weird. Which it was and is but I felt sort of like she was saying it of me, like I was weird, like what I'd been through had made me strange and different and broken. Which maybe it has, but it's not nice to think about and I tried to make my friend shut up. *We have to tell everyone, the guards and things*, she said, she kept on saying, in between *That's weird*s. I told her that we couldn't, and that it was okay and she should *shhh*. But still she told her mam, who rang my mam, who kind of smoothed it over, just a bit. I think she said that I was 'distraught' because of the split and saying things or something. Still, even though Mam knew, when she heard it from Anna's mam things seemed to click with her and we stayed there for a bit while we gathered things together and sorted all the hard stuff out.

If you want a photo or a particular thing, a poem scrawled up your leg in a specific font adorned with a cherry-blossom border, this will be designed, agreed upon, a stencil will be made and then it starts. If you want a Tweety Bird or Celtic cross on the small of your back, then that stencil would probably already be there, so it's faster.

Mam did go to the guards a few times on him. In the early days, she said. And once when I was small and he hit me by accident. It was rarely me he hit, and when he did he was usually pretty sorry after. They couldn't do very much to help us out. There's this kind of reluctance to come inside a family and sort them out. I don't know the ins and outs of it. I hate that phrase 'the ins and outs'. It reduces everything to *that*.

I cannot wait to know the codes, to know the things that people who tattoo say to each other: 'I have to get some flash' or 'Have you seen the newest batch of flash?' Does flash come in a batch? Do people say that? Words that don't belong make your tongue fat and other people notice. I want a place where I slip in and fit.

I don't know if I trust Anna very much, though. Which is why I've blocked her on some things, not on others. I only reply sometimes when she messages. I trust her more than Tom. At least I told her. But when I did, it was kind of a thing I was still stuck in, I mean. I felt so hopeless about it. Mam kept promising that she would try to leave, but it was always soon and never now. I told her what he was doing to me and she went bananas and started packing and sat down and stood up again. But the thing is, she knew, she had to know. It was hidden, but there were things that should have been her clues. We weren't allowed to have a lock on the bathroom door. So he could pop in at any moment. I tried a few things – sleeping under my bed, putting my desk up against the bedroom door. Stuff like that. It didn't start all at once. It wasn't even every night or whatever, maybe once or twice every couple of months. It was hard for him to find the time. Mam didn't have much of a social life, and evil as he was, he still had enough shame in him to do the things he did to me in secret.

He eased up on her, but not so much that she'd suspect. He let her start going to aqua-aerobics at the gym. He said it was because her body disgusted him. Really it was not because of that. I don't understand it. But that's the way the Great Sky Bear rolls. Humans are perverse. We're ruining the planet just by living on it.

An autoclave's for sterilising things. It is big and clean-looking and you use it in hospitals and laboratories as well as places where tattoos and piercings are performed upon the body.

I like to read about things that other people have been through, child soldiers, people who got sex-trafficked, refugees and so on. It puts what I've been through in context. It could be worse. It could still be happening. Or I could be in a country where chocolate bars were in short supply. Not that I eat my sadness away. But it's good to have the option.

I wonder if I were fatter or so skinny that I grew hair all over my body, would it change things? Or if I could just turn into a bear. When I die, I imagine myself as a solitary sky bear, lonely like a god but without the responsibility of a god. I would hate to be pinned up there, like a specimen in biology, watching helpless as girl after girl repeated my mistakes.

Because there were mistakes too, I am certain. Things I did that I should not have done. Maybe I should have made myself more ugly. Maybe I should have screamed and screamed and screamed and told the world.

Steam not air is used to clean the tools within the autoclave. Hot air is less sterile than steam. The air needs to be taken out completely. Before the cleaning starts.

Maybe I should have stabbed him with a knife. I had one under my mattress for a while, but I always chickened out before I used it. He would have deserved it, though. And we would be better off financially, if I had killed him. Because Mam would probably have gotten everything. And with the money to pay for a good lawyer, maybe I would not have had to go to jail? Maybe just for *loads* of counselling or something. I don't know much about the law, but if it was self-defence or not-wanting-to-get-rapedness or something, I think that that is mitigating.

I am changing my name by deed poll as soon as I hit eighteen. My friends here call me Ces, to rhyme with chess. Sometimes, in my other school, people tried to call me Fran, to rhyme with man. I didn't answer. I have the same name as my dad, only in feminine, *e* instead of *i*. He was bossy like that. Mam wanted to call me Catherine. I think I like that. I could be a Catherine, I think. Like

Granny Kate who's dead. A Cat. A Cat would suit me fine. There is this story that I used to have about a Cat who Walked by Himself. I'd like to be a Catherine, a girl who needed no-one. Nobody at all except myself. Not as much as I'd like my dad to die, but you can't have it all.

You use them in hospitals to neutralise waste, so when you throw it out it won't infect anybody else. Our bodies can catch illnesses so easily. Even things that are sterile in the body carry horrors when they are released.

Before I sleep, I spin my father's story. He is in the doctor's office and they find a tumour deep within the meat of him, his reproductive organs to be specific. It has to be cut off and he has to take all these hormones so he won't grow breasts and lose his hair. He does anyway. Also, he gets bitten by a rat. A wild rat. Wild rats' bites are poison, really dirty. They can kill you. Apparently you die in agony as well. It was Dad himself who told me that when I was very small and so I know he'll know what to expect. Anticipation heightens things like terror. I would like my dad to feel afraid and helpless, trapped within a body he can't fix that's eating him, that's chewing him to pieces.

I would like an autoclave for people and their thoughts.

Applied pressure, forcing me to purify myself. In a while I'll rise up like a phoenix, bursting from the girl that I am now. I will become a wholly different woman, independent and invulnerable, who cannot fathom all the sadness and the anger that she once held inside.

I sleep the softest ever sleep. The sleep that people sleep when they are small and have had a big aul' day. I probably snore all the live-long night. My nose is still blocked up, the air comes in my mouth and that is noisy. My face is sore, I can feel all the places under skin and inside bone. Cavities in cheeks and nose and forehead. The ones you never feel until they fill.

I would go through fire to feel that way, flay off my skin, dance on hot coals or on broken glass like girls in fairy stories. I want to rewrite the language of my body, the tension and repulsion in my bones.

We need help. Financial help and other kinds as well. Mam more so than me but if she dried out, like, went somewhere for weeks and weeks and weeks, I would be on my own and I don't know how safe that would be. With no-one to take care of would I do much better or much worse? Would I drift into myself and live in filth like she does?

She needs me and I need her. And I'm not sure who needs who more because neither of us is good at being people. It's just we're bad in complementary ways.

'I love you, Ces,' she says sometimes and pets my hair when I am in my bed or on the sofa. 'I love you, Ces. We're safe now.'

I think she says it more for her than me.

People think that psychological scars are mental only. Patently they're not, as anybody knows who breaks out in a sweat when they hear certain voices, scent certain odours on the air. Sense and memory can help each other out, link thing to thing.

To ease a sin, you first must be contrite, then say it out and then do something to make up for it. I felt that sex with Tom was my contrition, but I have not had my absolution yet. Maybe that will come with proper love. But in other places, penance is an act of hardship. Something harder to go through than rosaries. Fasting, sleeping on a hard stone floor, immersing oneself over and over again in water till you lose your breath and nearly drown. I could do such things, I have done. I tried to stop eating for a week once. Made it to day two, then gorged myself on deli chicken pie. I'd do it if I knew that it would work, would flush out all my sin.

Burning would be a good way to go for Dad. They used to burn witches and he's worse. A phoenix lives for aeons. When it's old it goes into a fire and it burns and then it is reborn from the ashes. They are fire colours – golden, red, orange, yellow. Vermilion, scarlet, ochre, burnished poppy. If Dad were put to death for what he did and burned alive as people never were for raping women, could I mount the pyre and burn too and come out whole, just a baby, fresh and blinking?

I don't feel whole. I feel like a charity-shop jigsaw, missing bits and with some bits that don't come from myself but were put inside my box from other jigsaws and I do not like it.

I never enjoyed jigsaws, I always wanted to make my own pictures. Even when I copied things exactly, I liked to be the hand that held the pencil. Making things from lines and curves and colours. Mam likes them, they're repetitive. She used to do mine for me when I was little. I'd always get a few at Christmas and get sick of them after a bit and she would finish them off painstakingly, piece by piece, and then she'd break them up and put them back inside their box inside the press where we kept toys and games. I had a lot. My dad gave us a lot.

Not all tattoos are symbolic, some are medical. Or traumatic. Underneath the skin a stain can cling. Even when unwanted. Gravel from a car-crash on a road. Coal-dust from a mine. These things can print you with unchosen signs that people see. The mark can be forced in.

There is a cat in the back garden eating a bird. A little sparrow. Brown. I like the shape of its body and I'm trying to sketch it. I like birds. Fat little sparrows. They look content. And I suppose they are until they pounce. I wonder if the cat belongs to anyone. And if it does, if it knows that it's owned. I think that feeling might shame a cat and make it angry. It's probably a little angry all the time to want to kill things. A little cold. I snort the snot back inside my throat and swallow. There are tissues, but they're far away.

Something that
you'll probably regret

Freeze the skin of the pig in a bag until you need it. It is best to strap it to a body, warm and real. So you'll get the sense of actually doing what you want to.

I love you.

Stretch it out. It's not the same as human skin at all, not really. But it's close enough.

Shhh.

I wish my skin was thicker. My pain threshold kite-high, ready for anything or nothing.

Don't cry.

Pigs squeal easily, but mostly out of fright.

Don't listen to your mother.

They cannot sweat. Would humans sweat? I wonder as I push the needle in and start my work.

You're my best friend.

Pig skin can still burn in the sun, so piggies must rest careful in the shade and clothe themselves in mud for their protection.

You'll be all right before you get married.

Their tails can be curly, straight or wavy, like our hair. Their penises are corkscrews, digging in, opening and piercing.

Sure, who'd have you?

Female pigs breed better when they enjoy it, studies have explained. I am oddly pleased by this.

Your mother is depressing.

My grandmother had pigs when I was young and I would touch them sometimes, reaching out into their pen, half-frightened, half-enthralled.

You look just like your mother when you're whining.

I always wanted to draw on them, to dress them up in wild fantastic colours. Their dead skin occasionally makes me feel guilty and ashamed.

You've brains to burn – you don't get that from her, that's all from me.

When released, they forage and invade, these pigs, they survive and thrive in the wildest of places, making space their own. Finding food and breeding with each other, raising babies, snuffling in the grass.

Once upon a time there was a little girl …

Gullinbursti was a golden boar who belonged to Freyr, who was a god.

Come here, pet.

I read it in the grey book when I was small. It might have been my favourite. Mostly for the pictures.

Happy birthday.

Freyr challenges dwarves to make him a gold pig and they do.

Happy Christmas.

I would like a gold pig of my own, I thought to my child self. The guild of dolls did little to protect me.

Happy Valentine's Day.

At first I wasn't sure what he was up to, but I knew it made me feel discomfort in my skin and in my body, even when he was finished.

I got you something.

Touching at first, and as the courtship proceeded making me touch him, and other things and other things and other things.

I hope you like it.

I was twelve.

When I was small, your gran would take me to the zoo in Dublin.

Squealing like a pig the first time, after that silent. Unclean and inedible to anyone outside my inner circle, the ones who made me and are supposed to love me. Nothing magic ever came to help me. Stories only stories and not real.

The two of us would get the bus, and bring a bag of sandwiches and a flask of tea. I'd only be allowed tea on a trip. Sweet for me. Your gran didn't take sugar.

Three little pigs and Wilbur from Charlotte's Web. *I should draw them on pigskin, to be funny. But the next project is close to my heart.*

And my favourite was always the chimpanzees.

A baby picture of me, eyes big and trusting, before my face grew and they remained the same.

Because they looked like people.

This is how I looked before I knew what the world really was, what living in it meant for girls like me.

With their fingers and their toes and their funny little faces.

I wish I was still little. Small enough to hide beneath my wardrobe with skeleton and machine, to cuddle into the laps of the remaining members of the guild.

You can put clothes on a pig, dress it up. But that doesn't make it a person. Ask your mother.

To blow up on the wind into the stars and cuddle up into a little seed, to cling eventually to the hot-cold fur of the glistening Sky Bear.

You're developing. Don't think I haven't noticed.

To track his fleas and pick them off to eat. To breathe in rhythm with his massive breath.

It's a father's job to teach you things. So let's sit down and tackle them stupid old sums. And we'll keep at it until you understand them.

To fly away sometimes, and draw things on the stars.

Do you feel better now?

The eye, the anchor, the heart, the angel wings, the spider in a web.

You'll make some lucky man so happy some day, sweetheart. Not like your mam with me.

To float back home and whisper to the Sky Bear of my day. The great flap of his ear a blanket. The rumbles of appreciation and of laughter.

If someone's hurt you, tell me and I'll fix it.

I'd always be sure to put some honey and other things bears like into my stories just to hold his interest.

Things my dad has said to me and meant.

If I had died inside my mam, maybe I could have had something like that. If the world were not the world but just a little story that I'd heard.

A COOL WAY TO BE HURT

Facial ones can mean you're in a gang or stuck in jail but there are other reasons for them too. People judge the face ones, but I like them. I don't give a fuck, your skin proclaims. I am a host for interesting things.

OK, now I know what Tom wanted. It was to dump me. This will not stand. I had no idea I would be so upset and there it is. I think there's someone else. He said there wasn't but I'm sure there was. Why else would he turn down the stringless touching thing? He said that he sensed that I wanted more than he could give. That he was going through some stuff. That I had no idea what life could be, that I was just a child. He gazed out the window like a man in a soap, who was breaking up with a woman in a soap. Then he offered to make me a cup of tea. I kind of begged him to reconsider, which was not in character and also very humiliating.

This kind of thing is literally the last thing that I need right now. I'm glad that I'm off school. Tom called over, early in the morning, said he was on his way to class. Which is totally not true, but he wanted an eject button, an excuse not to have to stay indefinitely, to keep things easy, nice and finite. I took his cup of tea and wondered for a horrid, fleeting instant whether now was the time to tell him about Dad. Would that make him stay with me for ever? No, but maybe it would work for, like, a month. Decided not to, though, because he would probably accuse me of being emotionally manipulative.

He said there was something about me that made him really angry. That I was not all there, but when I was he wasn't sure he liked me. That I was not really his type physically. Not all in a row – they came out when I started bickering at him, which was pointless really, because nagging isn't a good strategy to make someone realise that they shouldn't break up with you. Seducing him would have been more like it. But after all his words, I didn't want to.

Little by little, he polluted what we had with observations about things that are wrong with me. In dribs and drabs he ruined the us there was. Now the bad stuff is what I will remember. My head hurts and my heart hurts and my back hurts and I am full of things that I don't want.

Permanent make-up is a tattoo. It isn't really make-up. Sometimes, it isn't even permanent. It isn't ink exactly, what they use.

When Tom and I had sex. I need that feeling, I think, but I would like it best from only one person, because I do not want to sleep with loads of people until I am old enough to enjoy it properly and also am not living with my mam. Also, he lived so close. It was nice to have somewhere to escape to, away from school and home. Away from my real life. I am so busy and Tom is so not-busy. When I was at his house, I felt less busy. Like I could breathe and not worry about my next step.

It lasts for years, your eyebrows keep their shape. The arch will not wipe off with rain or sweat.

Mam is in her room as well today. I think she is asleep. It is three o'clock in the day. She must be having a bad day. I was pretty loud with the crying and so on. She didn't come in or anything, but that's kind of normal. What she does. She once told me that's because she thinks I need to be alone, but really it's because she is sick of having to deal with my drama.

But this whole thing is also kind of her fault. I mean, she had a choice, she married Dad. She didn't have to bring a child into this world to be raised by a psycho. I had no way out from day one. I know it's not her fault he did what he did, but it is her fault he got the opportunity to do so. Would you let a wife-beater babysit your kids? There is only one answer to that question if you are not a shitty person.

Black lines define eyelids. Needles on the thinnest weakest flaps of you but perfectly safe once it's hygienic. If needles aren't clean, if hands ungloved then you should start to worry. Things transfer and damage you. Make you sick to death or even ugly.

Horrid in a woman. In a man.

If you're doing it to someone, you need to be so careful of their body. And of yours. You need to be so fresh and pure and wiped and cleaned and covered up with latex.

I wonder what my brother would have been like. I never got to see him, in the end. I asked to but they didn't think that it would have been right. By that stage I had seen a lot worse, so there probably would not have been that much harm in it. He would be eight now. And probably royally messed up in the head from all the drama his short life had had. Even now he would not be immune.

We keep drink in the medicine press. When I went to get a Lemsip earlier, the whiskey was all gone. It is a classy drink as drinks go. The proper kind for someone to get drunk on. Initially her tipple of choice was Irish Knights, the knock-off cream liqueur you get in Lidl. She has used it in coffee, tea and hot chocolate sachets as an acceptable milk substitute. Next step, cereal. It is hilarious. Only it isn't really, is it? I liked the hot chocolate one best of all.

She likes me to drink with her sometimes, when she forgets to be a mother. It makes her feel less alone. Drinking alone is something she has always associated with alcoholism. Drinking with your child is, apparently, both fun-loving and socially acceptable.

She is a legend. Pity it is the legend of Baba Yaga, the witch who had a chicken house and ate children for lunch. Not that she's that bad. Dad is Dada Yaga, Mam is just desperately sad.

Livia told me about Baba Yaga once, when we were on a late. We swapped the messed-up stories that our people tell to children. I told her about the evil stepmother who turned her husband's children into swans. I looked up Baba Yaga later on. Her chicken-legged house had made me worried Livia was joking. She has a funny sense of humour sometimes.

Line by line a question-markish swoop, a nineteen-thirties

madam of an eyebrow. I wonder if a person's ever wanted
one that's raised to permanently judge the world and find
it wanting. Eyebrows tell us things. They raise and furrow.
Manipulate our foreheads, crease and wrinkle them like
dirty sheets.

I am sad as well, but I have the busy-ness to distract
me from the sadness. When Tom left, I did something
quite stupid that I haven't done for ages. I opened up
Black Doll. She has a stitch near her flat crotch, right up
under her skirt. And out of her I pulled my little wooden-
handled knife. I drew a red road right up my tummy, up
and down, from crotch to just below my breasts. Like
a surgeon. Then I flicked line after line across to make
up stitches, like a drawn-on scar on a child's picture of
Frankenstein's monster. I felt like plunging all my hand
inside, taking out my stupid, stupid heart and just
destroying it, squashing it beneath my heavy feet, biting
and chewing at it with my teeth that are a little crowded
but we can't afford an orthodontist, sorry. I wish that we
could give you more, you can't and no-one can and no-
one's going to, not even me, not even if I live to be a
hundred.

You can tattoo eyes and eyebrows. You can tattoo lips and
softer places. People often have new nipples made. It isn't

hard. It's one of those instances where even the traditional don't mind it. It's seen as fixing. A return to form.

I haven't cut myself in ages. I sometimes get the urge to, but usually I suppress it and just draw something. I have a baby picture of myself that I've sketched out. I'm just perfecting details, deciding where I'm going to draw it on.

There's something really sad about looking at children. I mean, they are so easy to destroy. All it takes is words if you are good with words. A child will love you no matter what. They don't know any better, do they, children? They don't know that Mam and Dad are people and that people suck and always disappoint you in the end.

I wonder if I could get Tom done for statutory rape? I was only fifteen when we had sex for the first time. He told me I was beautiful and nobody else had told me that. I liked hearing it. Of course again, there were the other things. The 'You're ugly when you're crying' one that stung particularly hard, because I spend so much of my time trying not to cry and when I do, the last thing that I need is to be part of some beauty contest where the participants are other, less ugly versions of myself.

You can make them 3D just with colour. Light and shade. An erect illusion. Or if you want the feel of them to work, a surgeon makes a knot of skin and once that's healed the artist comes to pink it or red or brown it.

I have amassed a lot of unnecessary experiences for somebody of my tender years. Once I'm eighteen I can go on the dole, get my own flat and maybe get a job that doesn't involve slicing ham all day. People love ham here – nobody is Jewish, I assume. I've never met a Jew. The same people that eat all the ham would probably be sickened by my bloodied squares of skin and my machine. It is the only thing about me that is marginally normal. I have a hobby. Like an Enid Blyton character. Soon, a kindly uncle and an unexpected adventure!

That also sounds like a tagline for an incest movie, though. Not that there are a lot of incest comedies out there. It is the kind of thing people don't really find funny except in the context of an off-colour joke, and then it is mainly the offensiveness rather than the actual imagery that is hilarious.

I sometimes wonder if my friends really like me. I've gotten a few, 'ow r u feelin?' messages from Joanne and some properly spelled ones from Sheila, who puts commas and quotation marks in everything she writes that seems to need them. I've replied with some under-the-weather-looking emojis, mixed with happy ones because I'm not at school. They think I am their friend but they don't know me. I am what I have been through as well as what I am. And, while I would hate to let the stuff that was done to me define me, I sometimes feel that it kind of does. I worry that I'll always hate everybody. Up to and including myself. Especially myself.

There are many, many different shades. With soft and paintish names. Strawberry patch. Delicate blush. Cappuccino. You can change the colour you were born with if you want. It's up to you. You're glad to be alive. So live a little.

I have so many coping mechanisms that sometimes I feel like a robot – no soul, all function.

Today I'm functionless. Mostly, all I think about is Tom. I stay in bed. At some point Laura leaves the house. When I do get up there are hazelnut yoghurts in the fridge and extra-special fancy biscuits and soft bread. Comfort food. She must have heard me crying because she does not like yoghurt herself. Because she craved it when she was pregnant with my brother, and it reminds her of him. She hated the smell of baby-related products for a while. She doesn't like that aisle in the supermarket, even now. But once, even though she'd have to show Dad the receipt and the purchase made no sense and he'd get angry, she bought a tin of SMA and looked at it and cried and cried and cried. I put my head on her shoulder and put her arms around me and mine around her, and her eyes said it was not the same. She would have had me anyway, you see. I must have been, like, seven, maybe eight, because it was soon enough after and I was pretty small, I came up to her shoulder when she was sitting down. I had to go on tiptoe to get my head on it as I recall. After a while, my neck began to hurt, so I peeled our arms apart and tiptoed off. She was still crying.

Nobody in our family can fix anything. Even when they try to, things stay broken.

You don't have to limit it to nature. There's a spectrum. Neon. Vibrant. You could have a sci-fi pair. Surprise prospective lovers. Size is another thing that's up to you, your nipples could be blankets, brightly cloaking where your breasts once lived.

Mam can't even change a light-bulb. Dad used to do all that stuff, and now I do. I clean the filters in the washing machine. If it is more complicated, we call the landlady. I would like to have a toolbox. I have a pliers, but I kind of need a hammer and a wrench as well – they would come in very handy.

I had a screwdriver in the old house, from when I tried to put a lock on my door. Dad broke one of Mam's fingers the next day. He took it off and I never replaced it. If he had broken one of mine I could have gone to the police or something. But if he hurt someone else, it just seems cruel to labour the point. He wasn't at his worst back then, but the way he looked at me was creepy and when we were in the house alone he would ask me to sit on his lap and wiggle, or press himself against me rubbing up and down up and down, whispering disgusting things in my ear.

I hated him. I hated him. I hate him. But hating him means hating part of me as well, I wish I could cut out half of myself, but Mam's half isn't something to be very pleased with either. Would it be less disgusting, my history, if I had been adopted? Would I loathe myself less? It seems possible, but wishing doesn't change things that can't change.

Some women do not want to change right back and they get different marks they choose instead. Celtic crosses, weaving like a crop top. A flowerbed on the soft and flat that used to dip and rise. Victorians used to make their flowers mean things.

I need to rewire myself, to find something that will make it OK. I leaned a bit on Tom to help me find some pleasure in my body, in myself. If I could make him laugh, if I could make him want me, maybe that would mean that I was clean, that I was normal, that I was worth saving. It is not up to him to save me, obviously. I mean, what from? It's not like there are dragons after me or that I am in danger.

I need myself to save me from myself. Which is a challenge, because being me is what is dangerous at the moment. The things I have been through have given me impulses that should be resisted. Cutting myself, for example. Eating too much and then forcing my fingers down my throat, tickling and pressing on my epiglottis till I feel the wave and throwing all the horror of it up. I do not do this every day. Just sometimes, when I kind of cannot stop myself from eating. Twelve slices of toast with butter, several chocolate bars, a bag of sweets and all the greed and all the wasted money just confronts me in my head and so I need to be punished, deserve to be hurt.

Tom once brought me a blue hydrangea. He took it from a garden that he walked past. I kept it in a jam jar by my bed. I draw a blue hydrangea and a purple and a pink. They change, you know, depending on the soil. On where they're put. Like me. Hydrangeas have two meanings. I looked them up a while after it died. They can mean heartfelt or heartless. Also frigid, but that doesn't apply. I don't think Tom had thought it through like that. It probably meant: *Here is a thing. I like you. Here's a flower.*

Something inside me wants to hurt me badly and it creeps out like a goblin when I let myself down. It's not that it isn't me who's doing it, because it is. It always has been me who does these things. But I spend so much time inside my head, pretending that I don't live in my body, that I am far above it or below, in the soft earth where all the pink and grey and wiggly soft things co-exist unimportantly together. It would be warm below, unlike the Sky Bear's territory. The bear himself would be quite warm, he is a deity but also a mammal so the blood inside him warms his bearish star-bones. But in the earth, you would not need to cuddle into bears to warm your skin. The earth would cuddle you, damp and tepid and inordinately comforting. Water in it would drip in your mouth and sometimes there'd be rabbits in it also. Will it be like that when I am dead, I wonder? On days like this I think I'll be dead soon.

St Bridget is the second biggest saint we learn in school, alongside Patrick. February is hers and we made crosses out of rushes every year until I left primary school. I liked it, doing things with my two hands – repetitive but also making something. It calmed me down a bit like drawing does.

On the sofa I sit and eat yoghurt with a small spoon. I do not want it really, I'm not hungry, but it slides down my sore throat so easily. It tastes sweet and substantial. Nuts are full of fat, but it is good fat, the building kind that people actually need.

Bridget wanted land to build a convent. And she asked

the king and he said no and so she prayed. Praying's like
a weapon that saints have in the old stories. It makes you
strong. It makes you like a wizard.

My toes itch today and Tom is somewhere, being smug
and glad that he has checked me off his list. There is a girl
he likes, I think, in college. He went to see her acting in a
play and didn't ask me to come see it with him. But then
again, we didn't really date. Did he think of me as his
girlfriend, then, that he had to break up with me? Were we
a couple? I don't really think so, but who knows what goes
on in someone's head? I hate the idea of him preferring
someone else to me, even though I cannot fault him for
that. She probably is better than me. A lot of people are.
Most everyone. My suspicious mind keeps turning it over
and over as though it were a problem I could solve. An
equation I could balance. A theorem I could prove.

I'm going to be so behind in maths. I hardly understand
it when I'm there.

I draw a stained-glass face with massive shining eyes and
long brown hair, rush-thick, that weaves in crosses.

I hope that I'll be better by tomorrow, because I really
need to go to work. I have the early shift – six AM till half
past twelve. It isn't open until seven, but there's cleaning,

papers to be sorted, pre-made pastries to put in the oven, salads to put out, ham to slice. There's always ham to slice. If I grow up to be a tattoo artist like I want and I am really famous, I bet all of a sudden there will be ham slicing involved in the profession. Wafer-thin slices of ham prepared fresh while you get inked. I hate when people say, *Look at my ink*. Also, *Check out my tat*. That is even worse, because it sounds like *twat*, which is disgusting.

I want to do it for people who do it for the love and not for notice. It is OK for someone to be proud, but it should be for them, not some sort of way to emblazon the idea that one is alternative or tough or whatever.

I wonder what my tattoo will be when I decide to get one. Something that reminds me of purity and strength, perhaps. Diana. Athena. Morrígan. Macha. Méadhbh. Or a sleeve of all of them at play. There are strong women in the stories of every culture, but I need to find the one who is for me, the one who could guide me towards a sort of peace when my breath stops in my throat and all I want to do is not exist.

My favourite one is Macha at the moment. She was a horse goddess, hurt by men who made her lose a baby. She was hurt and she took her revenge and hurt them back. I like revengers. They make me kind of happy. I wonder how many famous stories of revenge there are. How many vengeful women would weave together all around an arm. I need to make a list and start to sketch.

The king relented, but only a little. He said he'd give her all that her cloak covered. She took it off and shook and shook and shook it and it covered acre upon acre. And he knew that she was someone he should not annoy and so he did what he was told and knelt before her.

The first tattoo I ever saw was on the bald head of a man on the bus. I was going to town with Laura. (She doesn't have a car, she cannot drive. Dad didn't want her to learn. Where would she go that he could not come too? he thought. Now it is a problem, getting to work, getting back from work.) The drawing was a snake that curled around the back of his pink head, the only bit of it that didn't gleam. It was dark, the mouth and tongue were red, the lines between the scales were a lighter blue than the scales themselves. Mam told me to stop staring but I couldn't. The idea that someone could be drawn on like that made me so excited and afraid. I wondered if the man wanted that drawn on his head. Did he know? Should we go and tell him? Mam pulled me away, already sick of my little questions.

Bridget was a badass, like the old gods. People say that she came from a pagan goddess. The church took one of ours and made it theirs. Syncretism it's called. They did it loads. Taking what they wanted for themselves. I feel like I'm a pagan, if I'm anything. Worshipping my bear, the one I chose.

I wasn't a very verbal child, but when I saw that, something in me leaped. From then on, when I looked at picturebooks I saw them as possible drawings on places on people. The tiger who came to tea between the shoulder-blades of a very pretty back. The gorilla swinging from leg to hairy leg. The wild things round a wrist, nudging excitedly at each other. Sara Crewe reaching up a spine, with currant buns.

I didn't read that much until I was, like, ten; then I took off. I always liked to be read to. And I loved the pictures, different styles to match the different stories. Mam loves children's stories as well. Except that poem, the one about the birds. *One named Peter, one named Paul.* They used to sit on walls together, and then they flew away. When Mam said, *Come back Peter, come back Paul,* I distinctly remember a tremble in her voice that alarmed me and made me think the blackbirds were both dead. I knew what dead was because of the goldfish in our classroom. They kept on dying, floating to the top of the tank, so limp and elegant. Birds could die – I'd seen them on the road. And dying made people sad. Ergo Peter and Paul had to be dead. Why else would Mam's voice go all high and low like that?

I draw a telegraph wire with no birds. A feather floats towards it from a higher bit of sky. It could be Paul's, but in my head it belongs to Peter. Peter has just been eaten by a hawk. Paul is for dessert, beating his tiny wings at ninety miles an hour trying to fly away away away from being eaten. And maybe he will, but I don't think I will.

Come back Paul, says Death. *Have you met Peter?*

I sometimes think that life will eat me up and spit out the gristly ends of me that are worth nothing.

Even though there's more to Bridget, when they warped her, God became her boss. Chastity and things became important. Pagans don't have bosses. Or not so many.

I can see myself when I am Mam's age, just like her but even worse. Or dead. I wash the dishes she left from last night. The cat is lurking by the bins, watching for Peter, or possibly Paul. I pour a saucer of milk for it and leave it by the door. It hisses at me, but when I check back later, the milk is gone, so something must have drunk it.

Lying on my back I feel the edges of the world blur around me. I am so tired, sick and broken hearted. I still need to hoover. I don't know if I'll bother to go to work tomorrow. I don't know if I'll go back to school. Everything seems really dulled and blunted – pointless but still sharp enough to wound.

It isn't sinful but it feels like sin. I'm not. Sinful. I cannot help it but you cannot keep on fighting it indefinitely.

After time, it just becomes a chore. Empty the machine and pair the socks. Like that.

But not like that.

Here is one I learned from my gran. Bridget wasn't going to marry because of God. People didn't like that. Wasn't normal. One man came and laughed at her and teased her, saying that her eyes were very lovely and they would ensure she was betrothed despite herself. She shoved her saintly hand into her socket, pulled her eye out and offered it to him. 'For who would have a blind girl?' Bridget said.

I'm still off. The school rang. But I'm sick. The kind of sick where you need looking after. There isn't anybody here to look.

Feet ache but I get up and do all the jobs. Then I go to sleep. I cry before I sleep. I do not sleep until I'm tired of crying. I'm tired, I'm so tired. I am wrecked. Later on, I see the black cat stretched on top of the coal bunker eating a hard-boiled egg, complete with shell. Where did you get that egg, silly cat?

Gran rings, which is a rare occurrence. It's a short and awkward conversation.

'How are you?' Her voice is high with nice. She's making such an effort just to stand me.

I say, 'OK.'

'And how is school?'

(We're fine. We're fine without you.)

She says some things and trails off. She needs to see us. I don't know how to respond to that at all.

'Can it be next week?' I ask. Or later.

She doesn't hear. She's got the whole thing planned. Of course she does. She is coming over to stay two nights or so. She is going to stay in a hotel because she doesn't want to impose.

This is a good thing too. I want her to think that we are functional, so the less she sees of us the better, really. She will arrive, with Uncle Mark, tomorrow. I do not know why she is bringing him. For back-up, I suppose. At least he is not Dad.

And then she threatened him with bursting eyes. Is it still a threat if it came true? His eyes burst in his head. I do not know if I would like that power. So many eyes to burst. Such things to pluck. I draw an eye, cupped in a callused hand.

Uncle Mark is Dad's little brother. Not so little, big. He has two sons and a daughter and none of them seem scared of him at all. His wife, Claire, is the boss. She deals with Gran as if she were an equal. She does not defer to her at all. Gran does not like this, but she respects it.

Claire is staying at home with the kids. But for some

reason the olive branch is being extended now, and we need to sort out how we can accept it without revealing just how weak we are in terms of coping. Gran told Laura that she was a liar when she intimated what had happened to me. Me as well, although I 'had been coached'. We didn't spell it out. It is hard to do that to a mother. A mother wants her child to be perfect and nobody gets that so they settle for perfection in their eyes – or not being a dick.

Everything about Dad could be used as a weapon – his cruelties and kindnesses, his humour and his strength. Woe betide you if he pitted this against you.

Are cats even supposed to eat boiled eggs? It looks really incongruous. I text Mam and get stuck in to tidying and cleaning. This is not going to bode well for my flu, but I want to kill the squalor. Show them that our house is neat as pins, as shiny clean as fresh tattooing needles. Sanitised and safe. That Mam provides. That I am really good, when someone gives me the chance to be myself.

I draw a one-eyed woman in a cloak and she is lovely, bleeding from her face and almost smiling.

I make a lasagne for the freezer. Layers of things. A shepherd's pie as well, because why not? Otherwise the mince would go off soon. I bake apple crumble. I like these dishes because they offer homely comfort. Not that I can really identify with that, but so I've heard. They taste heavy and good inside my belly. I also make custard from scratch. On the cracks I stick some of my drawings in cheap picture frames, over photographs Mam brought with her when we moved away.

The pictures I stick up are these: a black-and-white sketch of a ballerina, leg extended, arm curved to the right, as though about to bow swoopingly to the floor; a blue and red and yellow picture of a stained-glass-looking tiger; a winking lady; and the baby sketch. They are not all the ones that I am proudest of but some of the colours match and I don't think they're offensive as the eye-cakes and hot zombies. The angel with the crow wings I stick on my wall. I drew him the week we moved in, when I was reading a romance about angels. He gazes down with sadness and no lust.

I like the idea of angels. I saw this film once where they had no genitals at all, just smooth and safe as Ken dolls. That would be a nice surprise, I think. Nothing looming like a threat. I always thought it odd that those could move – penises not angels – twitch up and down sometimes to even gentle touches. Sometimes, Tom says, it is inadvertent, but you can make it jump a bit if you concentrate as well. I miss having somebody to ask the weird things that occur to me. It's nice to know, you know. Amass these things. Information, like. It is a power. Not a very useful one, but still.

I begin to make a stencil. I have several ones already there. I need to decide quick before it rots and starts to smell. I think I'll carve my Bridget onto little flaps of pigskin. Cold and bloody.

My cold won't shake. It's been here ages now. Bundled up heavy, I go to the supermarket and get fresh tea-lights. If the room is lit with lots of tea-lights maybe it will be a bit less shabby. I'm glad we had the other ingredients in, because I have no money in my purse after I buy the lights. I go into Mam's room and hang up all her clothes. They litter the floor. I separate the dirty ones, the tights and bras and knickers, and put on a dark wash and hang it out. I load up a white one but can't turn it on because there is no space on the line till the darks are dry. There is so much to clean. They'll come tomorrow.

I'll pray to the Sky Bear that the little flaps of skin grow and grow so I can blanket them with all my pieces. I draw the bear. Performing bearish miracles, nebulas reflecting in his eyes.

I am small. Not small like children are. But smaller

than an adult. I'm not grown. My shape is like a woman's but it isn't. Curves and stretches small and only coming.

I was smaller then than I am now but when it comes at night it's like it's happening again, again.

My body feels the panic so immediate. I cannot handle this, it's wrong, it's wrong. It's not a thing that other girls do they're different to me I cannot take it squinting out the light until I'm blind.

A man is heavy on a woman's body. I am smaller all the air squeezed out. How can you fight off something that's inside you? Even when it's gone there is a wound.

Time and space are his, my noble Sky Bear. He'd never make a person's eyes explode.

And who would even miss me. If I left.

People get quotes sometimes. Different typefaces. Religious things. Or deep. More meaningful than normal. I don't know what I would get. I don't live by commandments.

Mam is scared of them. She sounds panicked. Voice is trailing up. She says that she will be home as soon as she can but it is late and still she is not here. I've done it all. She just assumes I have, she doesn't thank me. I sit at the kitchen table, picking Tipp-Ex off the shiny pine. At the back door there is a mewing. I open it and it is the black cat. He or she slinks past my feet and curls up underneath the table.

It could have fleas. I try to shoo it out. I text Joanne. She says when her cat Duchess had them, she scratched more often than usual. She sends a gif. This is not a help. I try to go over to the cat but it hisses at me evilly. Should I get it with the sweeping brush? I try but instead of going out the back door it jumps over the brush and out the kitchen door.

It does have a healthy-looking coat. Joanne says this is a good sign and that I should check its appetite. I mash up tuna and milk and put it on a saucer. We do not have a litter tray in the house. I narrow my eyes at the cat and wonder if I can get it out before it does something I'll regret. Waiting for it to emerge from behind the sofa, I bid Joanne goodbye. Perhaps I should have offered it an egg?

She is going to bring me my homework tomorrow, in the early afternoon in town. After her grinds. Then, visitors. I make a plan to go to bed early, but I don't know if it's feasible. I eat an orange and I watch the cat. Its eyes are supernatural-looking, when the slant of the light hits them in a certain deepened way. It doesn't like to be touched, this cat. It is burly and has one white sock. I think it looks like it could be a fighter.

O Bear, I kind of miss your presence in the world. Where are your cathedrals, your hymns?

I could get a little bear whose face looked up and little dots of tiny stars around him. Sky Bear from a distance. Survive beneath. Survive and eat your honey. Kindness wouldn't really matter to the Sky Bear, would it? But harming would have meaning. It would be a thing you did to stay alive. For you and yours. When bears attack, I don't think it's for fun. They're mostly shy of humans cause we hurt them. I'm mostly shy of humans too, I think.

I decide to put out the bins for the morning. When I return the cat is eating. As soon as it is finished, it scratches at the door to be let out. I would not want to stay here either. If I had my way, I'd slink out into the night to do my feline deeds.

I wonder what the world is like for animals at night. Joanne once saw a hedgehog in her garden. I've never seen a hedgehog, even once. In real life, I mean. When I was small I watched a lot of nature shows on telly, so I've seen them that way. They are funny little bags of fleas. Badgers like to eat them when they get the chance. Foxes pee on them to make them unroll their spines and when they do they get killed and eaten. Must be terrifying. I wonder if the hedgehog knows what's up when it begins.

I wonder if a cat would eat a hedgehog. I know a cat would eat a bird or mouse or pygmy shrew. Cats like meat, Joanne's cat Duchess often brings her gifts of little corpses. She writes them in her homework journal, kind of like a diary. Today a bird. Three days ago a rat. Joanne likes to record things that have happened as if they are important. She puts a red dot in the corner of the days she has her period. She doesn't tell us this, but one red dot a day for five or so days a month – what else could it be? Joanne does not really need to monitor her period, there is no chance that she could be pregnant. She hasn't even kissed a boy properly yet. I don't really feel like I have kissed a boy properly yet. Isn't that strange, a dirty girl like me?

Beware of humans.
Hide.
Survive.
Eat honey.
Protect your cubs. Don't let them hurt your cubs.

Mam hasn't come home yet. I ring Simon. She is staying over at his house. I'm mad she didn't tell me. I know exactly why, as well. She is scared of what Gran's visit means. She wants to hide. I want to show off how well we're doing by ourselves, without them. Her way might be more intelligent, come to think of it. I blow my nose again and again and again while I think about how messed up everything is. She probably met Simon after work and had a glass of wine at his house, made him have one too. He doesn't drive if he has taken even a small amount of drink. Simon tells me he will call her a taxi if I'm worried about being on my own when I am sick. I tell him not to be silly. I will be fine. I always have been fine. Worse things could happen.

The house seems very big when I hang up. I turn out the lights and close the doors, make sure the only radiator that's on is the one in my bedroom, time it for an hour, boil the kettle, fill a hot-water bottle for myself. Place it in my bed and change into my fleecy pyjamas with the owls on that I got from Gran two Christmases ago. I don't really grow or shrink. I kind of stay the same. Not big or small. Not ugly or pretty. Kind of fitting in with my mean little face that always looks like I'm thinking something unkind about the people and the world around me.

Text can loop and swirl or align weirdly. You can do fun things with it. Some people think that written words are boring for tattoos but I don't. What are they but shapes, like? I'd rather pretty words than ugly pictures.

Everything is ready for me to go to sleep. I make myself

a Lemsip to bring to bed with me, even though it means that I will have to get out of bed and brush my teeth. I stir a spoon of honey into it, almost text my Tom to say goodnight. He never was my Tom, though. Nobody can own another person. Even if they make them they don't own them. I have another yoghurt, my stomach feels real itchy where I cut it. I don't want to go to bed yet, so I put Dettol on it. It stings me really badly.

Under the couch and table is clean as a whistle, but maybe fleas are hiding in the crevices, all tiny and unseen like little bombs that will hop off tomorrow. So much could go wrong. So much is wrong already.

I lock the front door. Before I lock the back, I go out barefoot into the wet dark of the patch that forms our garden. In the dim I do not see the cat. I check the wall, the top of the coal bunker and underneath the bushes. It isn't anywhere. The cat is gone.

I go inside and put myself to bed and dream of crows that peck at saucers full of tuna, eyes and cream. I have to keep on feeding them or they will eat my eyes as well. I am working in a restaurant that caters exclusively to crows. The tuna surprise is our most popular dish, but there is also a ham slicer on the premises, in case the crows want ham instead of tuna. The eyes we get from corpses and from cats. We do not kill the cats, just throw them in a room all blind together. Their mewling plays over the intercom to hurry up our work.

Some time in the middle of the shift, I wake up to find my underpants are moist. I put my fingers down there and it's blood. I go out to the bathroom, slowly. Everything is eerier at night when no-one's home. Tension lurks around corners and in the shadow-pools of ordinary things. I get a pad in Mam's room. You are not supposed to use tampons at night for over eight hours. Or you might get toxic shock syndrome. I do not want this, although from the name of it, I might have it already. My life's a series of small and big shocks, most of them toxic.

I'm not used to a period just yet. It's still a foreign thing to me. A sort of marker. People want to get them. I never did but people want to get them. To be grown up. It means you can have babies and I don't want babies. I hate to think what I would do to babies. How I would try and fail and let them down.

People worship bears, you know, sometimes. I'm not the first. There are old carvings, pictures in museums. There are islands where bears mattered much. Once upon a time. Festivals and songs to worship bears. I cannot sing a song but I can draw. I draw St Bridget with the head of a bear. A spectacled bear. It takes me quite a while to get the fur right. Fur is hard to draw. If I'd that cat. If only it were tame, I'd shove it on the table and I'd sketch it. It wouldn't be luxurious as bears though. It wouldn't have a proper thick, like, pelt.

Tomorrow morning I am sleeping in. It isn't fair that I have had to do so much today when I am sick, when I should be in bed. The doctor said that I needed my rest. Clots of blood on toilet paper. I hope none got on sheets. I'd hate to have to change them.

I wash my face and brush my teeth again, just for something to do. Outside the window, yellow light and harsh. The grass looks grey, the moon a dirty smudge. I need to do the windows and the mirrors. If you go over them with newspaper they shine more brightly, not as many streaks.

The garden is free of hedgehogs. Slugs would love it here. No-one cares about it, nothing to eat them except for the odd bird, but not at night. We get some starlings here and also magpies. It's always mostly pigeons. It gets that way when you are in a town. I wonder where they go at night – the birdies, to their perches and their hidden nests. You do not see nests half as often as you do birds. But houses lurk everywhere. I pull the blind down on the catless garden. One by one my feet squeak me back to bed.

The Greek one, Artemis, could be a bear. There is a legend. She had a tame one, followed her around.

She showed it to people and some of them were girls, who stabbed it with their fingers till it bit. And then, of course, they killed it. Humans think they're more important than bears, than other things.

She plagued them then, the goddess, for a lesson. It wasn't in my book this one. I read it somewhere else, in an encyclopaedia we had in sixth class. We knew what virgins were by then and it was funny that there was a book that had them in inside our classroom. It got passed around.

You see the way to end the plague was offering virgins. Virgin means a girl in many stories. All the myths and legends. I read it and I wondered if I were Greek and it was olden days would I be fit to serve, and for how long?

I could draw that tableau on a back, all faded like a fresco or an old, old vase. I think it would be lovely. Sad and lovely.

A STORY ON YOUR SKIN
THAT HELPS YOU LIVE

To split a tongue in two and make it snake-like doesn't necessarily make you a liar. It's just a thing that people say, like two-faced. Serpent tongues are foreign, horrid things.

I wake, dress. It is still dark. Mam is out. I wonder where she is. I am not hungry and I need to go to work and get myself out of it early enough to go to town to meet Joanne. I just won't take my break. I wrap a woollen scarf around my neck and put on gloves. I should keep warm, I think. I don't want to be sick again. The house is clean. I will be home in time to meet Uncle Mark and Gran.

The morning is bright and clear, chilly and biting, but I am well-bundled in my jumper, hat and coat. Leaving the house I glimpse myself in windows. My legs look very thin compared to the fattened wedge that is my padded form. I look like a toddler or a boiler in a lagging jacket.

Work passes quickly, slicing things open, chatting

about Livia's new man. His name is Luca, and he has a pit-bull terrier. If they break up, which they will because Livia is always breaking up with people, she kind of wants to keep the dog. It's name is Bully, but it isn't one.

I butter some sandwiches, ready to be toasted. Turn on the coffee machine, face off the tins. Whoever was on last night restocked nothing. I hate that. All that stuff gets left to me because they know I'll do it. If you work hard all the time, people think that you like doing work. And I don't, but I need this job and so I do it properly.

It isn't easy to go through the process. The dividing. There is something jarring in the thought. You do it with a scalpel in a parlour. Avoiding arteries and veins, they cleanly slice. And cauterise it after. But there is another way as well.

Livia is wearing cat's-eye liquid liner and bright green eye-shadow. It gives her the look of a sexy cartoon witch. We talk about the dogs we'd like to have when we have lives and houses and aren't working in a dirty big newsagent's.

I grab some of the old trashy magazines from the break-room on my way out the door. Gran loves magazines, but only gets them sometimes because they are 'an indulgence'. I want her to think that we live a life full of indulgences now. The life that we deserve to have, if Karma was an actual real thing.

To do it by yourself, you must be brave and not a little stupid and impulsive.

It is hard to text or remove coins from my purse with fingers encased in gloves. Two pairs of tights and all my clothes mean I am sweating when I reach the centre of the town. Walking down the main street, I see three tattooed people. A lady with a butterfly alighting on a breast, a man with a star on the knuckle of his left index finger and a old guy with a tribal looking band around his wrist. I am perplexed by this. He does not look even the least bit tribal. Is it a token of the man he was or does he go home to a house filled with relics of primitive cultures? Beautiful pagan things that belong to the him he is inside. I wonder if he ever thinks about it that deeply. I would. I'll think and think before I get my first tattoo. I want it to be special. To mean something.

It's like the way that Sheila thinks about sex. She wants to be in love. So it's important.

I don't talk about tattooing with my friends at school that much. I kind of keep the things that matter close. If you tell people all the things you hope, they'll know when you don't get them and your disappointment filtered through their eyes will mirror back at you and make it harder. Like if you want an A in a test and tell everyone you're working for it, and then get a B. A B isn't a failure. But it is. Because you told those people and they know. Does that make sense? In my head it so does, but my brain's twisted over on itself like *pain aux raisins* or a Danish. Many of the premade pastries we half cook each morning kind of twist. I think it makes them pretty. Does anybody get tattoos of cakes? Maybe bakers do. Or pastry chefs.

When it has healed, you take a strand of strong nylon thread and wrap it through the hole, bisecting softly. Tighten it a little every day.

Waiting in the coffee-shop for Joanne to arrive I delete Tom's numbers from my phone. I had his home number there as well – he rang me from it once, early in the time we had together. It is calm, I have ordered tea and a scone. It is nice enough here. Pink things. Lots of doilies. I found some money in Mam's pockets yesterday when I was doing laundry and I have requisitioned it out of necessity. How bad would it look if I could not afford to buy a cup of tea? I mean, most people can. I usually can, but this week I have not worked, except for that one day, and so I'm kind of stuck. Fingers crossed it will all be all right.

Muscle breaks like bone but it takes work.

I should do babysitting, Joanne does it. It is easy work with only one or two. I used to babysit Mark's kids, Liam and Susan, now and then. They lived beside us in the old house. I don't really like children very much, but I liked *them*. We'd watch cartoons or bake and I'd stay over sometimes. Those nights were the best because I felt safe there, away from all the pressure at home. Mam liked to bitch about Dad all the time when he was away. She'd talk about how she shouldn't put up with this, and ask me what I thought, so she could throw it in his face later on. Not on purpose.

I stir the milk into the tea. It goes a pale brown and you can't see through it any more. Suspension to solution, our chemistry teacher would say. Or maybe she wouldn't. I'm not sure that I process what she says correctly most of the time. My scone is too dry and floury for my liking. I slather it with all the jam and butter I've been given and I wait. My book is in my bag and so is my pencil. I draw the teacup, and then embellish it with little stars and ivy with small flowers bursting from it. I write underneath it in copperplate a motto: *Behold the great cosmic teacup.*

Succubi would have forked tongues I think. They are the worst of demons, fiercely lovely.

The cupcakes here are prettier than scones: they are topped with sweets from when I was a child. Slices of refresher bar, jelly rings, fried eggs, alphabet sherbets, applejacks as well. Yum. Even the raisins in this thing are dry. I don't know how long they have had it out, but it tastes like the crap we sell in the newsagent's, pre-made and full of things to keep it from going bad.

I bet they sway on tiny little feet, legs as thin as twigs that snap in breezes. Hand-span waists and other lovely things.

I draw a cupcake, with little skulls to top it. The icing would be pink if I had my colours, but I don't. It doesn't look too bad. The skulls balance out the cutesy kind of well. I wonder who would want a bad-ass cupcake. A baking biker or a biking baker. A greedy pirating enthusiast?

They wouldn't show their lovers right away, they would wait until they hooked them in and separate their lips to suck the life right out.

The shop isn't packed, but most of the tables are taken up by the time Joanne gets here. She's red-faced and in jeans. She is one of those people who always seems a little breathless, constantly in hurries or about to do something of great importance. She is very organised and hands me my work in a coloured folder. I can keep the folder she says, which is nice. I thank her for the work and go through it bit by bit. Some of it's OK, but some's impossible. I think I will be OK to go back on Monday, even though I'm not exactly better yet.

She says that I look peaky.

I look at her.

'But then you're always pale.'

Huh. I didn't think of people thinking of me. Noticing the colour of my skin, my pallor or lack of. It unsettles me a little bit.

Slicing the tongue in two should not be done. Unless you have researched it. It needs a bit of knowledge to get right.

Joanne had maths and geography this morning; she is going back after lunch for accountancy, biology and French. She wants to be a doctor eventually and so she has to study really hard. It's not much of a life for her either this year, but at least she isn't completely emotionally destroyed by years of child abuse. She wants to look at my sketches and I let her, like they're not important. I can't pay for her food. She's doing me a favour but I can't.

She really likes them. She would get the cupcake tattoo if she were more adventurous. She says, 'I'd like a top, or, like, a dress. A little fifties dress with that print on it. Not a tattoo.'

I smile.

'Not that it isn't cute, but something on your body for forever. It has to be more special than cool. It has to, like, mean something.'

She rubs an errant raindrop from her cheek. I nod my head and we flick through the book and decide who would get what and why. It is lots of fun. She is sick of her friend Cally, who goes on and on about the boys she knows the whole time. They're friends but the kind where she is always telling her about fun things she and her friends have done but never invites Joanne along to do them. That would piss me off as well, if I were more into being friends with people, but now I am just glad to have people to talk to while I eat my lunch. Like a sort of human rain-jacket.

She says, 'I don't want to be paranoid or needy. But I want to, like, show her. By doing all of the things and having fun. Like, proper rockstar fun.' She does a sparkly movement with her fingers when she says 'rockstar'. Her hair is in a plait, she looks like she's twelve.

She says, 'I wish that I was more like you. Pale, and mysterious.' (Sparkle hands again, it must be her new thing.)

I remind her about the stressed-out cat text of the day before, which lacked mystery. She asks about the cat. I haven't seen it and I'm kind of disappointed that it didn't all of a sudden want to be my pet for some reason. I felt like I was being auditioned. And I failed.

She says, 'Having a cat is like that, a series of gruelling auditions, most of which you are destined to fail, but when you pass it makes it all the more special.'

She got Duchess on her twelfth birthday, the day her father died. The two events were separate but I think that makes her pet more special. She loves that cat a lot. I think if she were to get a tattoo it would probably be of Duchess. Perhaps wearing an Elizabethan ruff, for glamour and appeal.

She has to go. And I pay for my food and I walk home.

We need the tongue to speak, to mush up food and what if it goes wrong? You need for things to heal. You mustn't pick.

The place is kind of messy already, Mam has strewn her coat and scarf and bag on the floor of the hall. She is at the kitchen table drinking coffee and looking kind of grim. Her face is tired, the brackets round her mouth and under her eyes seem very deep, her pale hair harsh as light around her skin.

She asks me this: 'What did you say to Simon on the phone?'

I tell her I just wondered where she was. She stands up and stretches her neck out, approaching me, her face right up to mine. I can see the dry patches, the oily parts, the tiny little blackheads. She has a crop of them between her eyes.

'Simon's mine,' she says. 'He belongs to me. So you leave him alone and don't try any of your little tricks. Not this time.'

It does look terrifying, though, visceral. Like the scene in a horror film that makes you cover eyes.

It takes a beat for her words to hit me like a fist; and when they do, I feel the rage welling up inside me, blood in a needle rising, rising red and filling me and making all my hate burst to the surface.

I tell her shut up bitch and break a plate. And then I break another and another. Screaming that he raped me and she did nothing. She is a bad mother and a fucking victim. She won't bully me 'cause I won't let her. All the plates are broken now, and I don't care – she didn't even notice all the work I did to tidy up the house so Gran and Uncle Mark wouldn't have to see what a failure we are making of this life without him.

How dare she accuse me of stealing her man, when someone stole all the good in me and left me nothing, nothing! She took my fucking childhood and wasted it and threw it all away and now she's blaming me, and I want to punch her wobbly face so badly, to smash her stupid nose against the worktop, hold her down and make her see how much I've been fucked up and how complicit she was in that. She doesn't get to be a good mother all of a sudden. She doesn't get to tell me what to do. I have been nothing but good to her, have always tried my best since we got here. I go out to the garden and there's nothing there to hit and I come back in and go up to my room.

Systematically and with my two bare hands, I fuck the whole thing up, then I turn to the landing, her room and the bathroom and the stairs and the hall and sitting room and then the kitchen. Stamping and smashing all that I can find. I lock myself right in till Gran comes. Lamps gone, pictures on the floor, coat rack empty, blankets on the floor, I started out trying to tear them up but that is hard to do without a scissors so I settle for the appearance of mayhem.

I hear her crying and tidying and the sound is so familiar that I almost come out and help her till she yells upstairs: 'You're so like him, so like your fucking father that it breaks my heart in bits.'

I well up again and punch the walls until my hands are weak and bruising with it. I bite and rip my pillow, I can't believe her. I can't believe her. All the good in me was fucked right out and she just let it happen and she fucking knew, I saw her eyes I saw her eyes – she knew before she knew and now it's all breaking. I am broken and I'll never ever fix. I may as well be dead dead dead dead dead.

A HIDDEN PATCH OF SKIN

I am dreadfully squeamish about pretend violence. Gore. I kind of get much calmer when its real, I can watch it with a removed and neutral gaze, hard as a statue, able to get bandages and water, say the right thing. Cover up the wound.

At five o'clock exactly Gran's little silver hatchback pulls up. I see it from the curtains, peeping out. She parks it so exactly in the driveway, neat and tidy, fencing Laura in.

I put on shoes, I don't know when I took them off before, and look downstairs through bannisters, retreating. The smashedy bits are gone from the hall. It's almost tidy even if it isn't. The pictures back on walls. Uncle Mark opens Gran's door, she exits like a lady. Her feet are shod in dainty little heels. Gran won't wear flats, she thinks they are for peasants. Not that she would say peasants, but that is what her tone implies as her nose wrinkles. Women who don't try aren't worth much to Gran. The little blue coat, the little cream scarf, the little pink mouth and the little blue tinge in her perfectly set hair. Gran is, above all things, a lady. A hard thing with a soft shell.

Uncle Mark is in a rugby shirt and cords. His hair is kind of greasy-looking and he hasn't shaved. He's holding his hands in front of his crotch like a bouncer. I watch them approach the door tentatively and press the bell. Mam opens it and they don't come inside until they've talked a bit. I don't know what they say but she lets them in and calls me down the stairs as though nothing had happened at all just now, as though I were a girl and she were my mam and everything were normal. As though a visit was a visit and a house a home. I put my slippers on and pad downstairs to offer people tea.

We are jigsaws piece by piece so intricate, a slice or bump can hurt beyond repair.

The cat is on the coal bin again. This time he is not eating anything at all, but licking his paw and rubbing it over his fur. Rough tongues cats have. Wet pumice stones. The first time one licked me I was really freaked out by it. Cats rarely lick.

We never had a pet when I was small. I remember the tongue, but I have no idea whose cat it could have been. There were no pets because we could not be trusted to take care of them in any proper way. I never asked for one, even when I wanted one quite badly. I knew that something bad would happen to the pet eventually. It would be another hold over me, another thing I cared about.

Once I took a dying bird home. It was brown. I don't know what it was. It would have died anyway, but Dad snapped its little birdy neck because it was 'kinder than letting it suffer'. I don't know if it was all that much kinder, really. But I think he thought it was, he did not look cruel when he did it, more practical. I wanted to make it better. When things are sick and you are small that's what you want to happen. I was very scared that Mam would die that time she went to hospital to have the baby that was not a baby. After that, I always thought that she was something I should mind as well. Weak and fluttering, in need of protection.

Dad was pretty squeamish, he would cover his face during the road safety ads. I wonder how long it was before she stopped wanting to leave. Or if she never. It was a hurt she chose and didn't choose.

At the foot of the stairs I see Gran for the first time in almost a year. Uncle Mark looks big and awkward in our hall. His face is kind of crumpled, like a piece of paper scrunched up tight and then smoothed out but wrinkles still left in. Gran is doing most of the talking. Mam is smiling the smile she has that means *Move along folks nothing to see here – everything is fine if not idyllic.* I wonder can they tell that it isn't real, that that's not the way the real Mam smiles, the one that means she's actually happy. Her real grin cracks her face in two, it isn't lady-like. There is something surprised in it.

The lasagne is in the oven. There are other plates there now. I don't know where they're from, but she has them and the hall is reasonably tidy. We say, 'Hello,' 'Hello,' and I hug Gran. She smells like lady, clean clothes and perfume and talcum powder. We sit on the sofa that is covered with a floral throw. I wish I had left things the way they were. I wish I hadn't fought like that with Mam. She can't handle it. I forget that and get angry because she is supposed to be my mother as well as that. We are talking about work and school and all the polite things that people say. But things are swimming, silvery and pointed, underneath the surface. Fish that look like knives, or knives that look like fish. Cuttable and cutting.

Laura is embarrassed by what happened to me. *That* it happened, she didn't see it coming, and so it kind of has to be my fault, although it isn't. It is embarrassing, shameful and shaming. A dirty little secret only not so little in the context of our family or my life. My mother cast herself in the role of martyr, and she can't stand that I am the pig-faced daughter that she has to hide. Not all of me, but only some. I feel that I spend all my time in veils, like a princess in an eastern fairytale. You can see through the layers and layers of sheer fabric, but only the glimpses that cast me in a tantalising light. What normal people are. Without the veils the villagers run screaming, not for torches but to get away in case it might be catching. She wants the worst things he has ever done to be to her and it is hard for her to accept that in a way I had it worse. The sin done to me was bigger, more transgressive, more taboo.

Maybe not more hurtful, but who knows? Sometimes I don't think that I can hurt any more than I already do. And then Uncle Mark tells me: 'Your father laid his hands on little Susan.'

And everything goes red and spotted black, like my polka-dot skirt, only heartbreaking, and I am full of rage. *We told you*, I almost scream at Gran, but instead use the voice that is polite but not exactly polite. Like a gun with a silencer, lower but still full of murder.

'We tried to tell you. You didn't want to know, though. At the time. When it was only me he hurt, and Laura.'

She must have scars. He learned how to hit her where it didn't show. But she had moved to be with him and her friends drifted away one by one, like feathers off a duck that's being readied for a supper. I'm her little duckling, I suppose. I rather like to look at ducks and ducklings. They always seem so cheerful. Buttery meat on buttery bones cuddled up in multicoloured feathers.

But nobody told Uncle Mark, except that we had said some rotten things and Dad was going through a tough aul' time. He says they knew a little about Mam. But not the fullest extent of it. He had her on his lap. The wiggle game, she called it, just like me. It only happened once or twice and she felt dirty and she told her mam, just like me she told her mam. But her mam listened and she told her husband and he believed her too and she was heard. His big round face is serious as cancer. 'I want him jailed,' he says. 'I want to make him pay.'

When he talked to Gran she thought about the things that Mam had almost but not quite said to her that made her so, so angry at the time, but make her even madder now, but not with Mam, because if they are true she has to be more angry with my dad and with herself for not believing. She says, 'I am so sorry, Cessie love.'

I stare at her with dead-fish eyes and wish she would shut up so I could go to my room and think about what this means.

The ducks we know are mallards, We used to go and feed them, Mam and me. We'd take the bus with pockets full of bread we hadn't eaten. A mallard is a dabbling duck, she'd say to me and it would make me laugh, that sounds so weird. It means that it just dabbles in the water, mostly swimming on its surface. Between two worlds, not having to decide. But lots of things would like to eat the duck, not only humans. It is a very tasty treat for hungry beasts. A swan would be much harder to kill, I think. Do birds have little tongues or only beaks? I do not know. Donald Duck has a tongue but he is not a normal kind of duck, dressed as he is like a small sailor and spitting when he talks. His girlfriend has eyelashes. It is weird that people fancied Daisy. Shane Horan used to say that she was a bit sexy. At the time, I thought that meant pretty. I wonder what he thought it meant back then.

The oven dings, but no-one feels like eating. Uncle Mark says that he is so sorry for what I went through, but 'we have to make sure he gets what he deserves'. He means what he deserves for hurting Susan. No-one cared what he deserved for me. I say I'll set the table and get up and do it just for something to do. Uncle Mark is full of righteous anger, and I want to have a minute to myself before he tramples me with his high horse.

'We have to help each other,' he says. Words like 'stick together' and 'support'. But where were they before they needed us?

Sometimes people tattoo animals or babies. This is abuse, because a dog or cat or child cannot consent.

These plates are from Tom's house. I know because of all the toast I used to eat there once upon a time. Mam must have been desperate. I am stupidly angry with her for asking him for things, for letting him help out as if he were a decent human being when he is not. Or is but only sometimes. It's hard to know. I let myself be used and used him back as well and it was weird. I sometimes think I hate him, but I want to be his friend. Not for a while but some time, maybe maybe.

I need to stay away. And so does Mam.

I should not be thinking about Tom.

I'm pretty big on not doing things to things that are alive without consent.

I take the lasagne out of the oven with a thin tea towel instead of oven gloves. I get a little burned but not too badly. Not attention-seeking pain, more to help me focus. Gran's face is really old beneath her make-up. She wears lip-liner dark around her mouth and colours in between the lines so that it doesn't bleed into her wrinkles. I wonder if I'll ever do the same.

Uncle Mark is talking about sexual assault and

defilement of a child and I get the horrible feeling that at some point he is going to ask me who put what in where and when. Not that it is not on some level important that people know, but on another level it is horrible to talk about. It is private, but not in the way that other, nicer things are private. I look at him, expecting him to take out those dolls you see abused kids pointing to on crime procedurals. Where'd the bad man touch you? Show me, pet. He didn't care until it helped his daughter. He says he didn't know. I bet he did. He knew the story but his brain rewrote it. He blamed my mam for lying. He was wrong.

I do eat meat, though. Which I suppose is worse but also not. I mean, I don't think of my mince as saying no.

When they rang Dad in order to confront him, he asked them not to tell his girlfriend, like a child caught with sweets that were not paid for in a shop. Uncle Mark went straight to the guards, but you can't just arrest someone right away. There has to be paperwork and other things like statements. And when he went to talk to Gran about it, she told him about what Mam had said to her, and what it might have meant.

'I mean, it wasn't flat-out said. More *implied*,' she says.

Her tone of voice suggests that Mam should have flat-out said it, should have made her believe.

And then I go back in and raise my voice. Not rudely, just loud enough for all of them to hear me.

'You are my gran,' I say. 'Mam is scared of you because you were mean to her and always took Dad's part when they were fighting. What did you want to know? Where was she supposed to begin? You only had to turn your head and look, Gran. It's not like you can hide a thing that big? Why'd you think my baby brother died? Why'd you think I wet the fucking bed till I was twelve?'

I tell her that Dad kicked Mam in the tummy. I tell her that Dad kicked Mam in the face. I tell that he held her hand on the grill of the oven until she made a sound he wanted to hear. I tell her three and four and five more things.

'I could go on,' I say.

And then I do. All the things I say. About being eleven on your knees. About being older. Other things. About telling Mam. About leaving the only home I ever knew and feeling fucking blessed because it wasn't the kind of home at all that people should have. I cannot stem the talk from out my mouth that flows and flows and flows so quietly and decidedly.

My pig skin comes from pigs. Who didn't want to die. Their skin's a by-product though, like hooves or something.

A bit that would be wasted if not used. No-one kills a pig for just his skin. They want the meat, the juicy, tender stuff.

When I am finished, Gran is like a little broken doll. Like Blue Doll if you took out all her stuffing. Uncle Mark is harder to read. He is looking at me like he wants to ask me something. Saying that Dad 'has to pay'.

I stare him down and tell him: 'You only want my dad to pay for Susan. But for that you wouldn't even be here. And nor would Gran. You both chose Dad. And Dad, he was the bad guy in all this and now you want us to join your justice team. So self-righteous. You aren't though. It's selfish what you want from me and why.'

They try to say things but they stop and I breathe in and Mam can feel me working myself up, and possibly she is thinking of Tom's plates because she says that that's enough and hugs me from behind. Her clavicle is hard against my shoulder. My little bony mother tries her best.

I offer them both tea again, but nobody wants tea. It is hard to talk about all this, but once you start a bit it is hard to stop. This is the danger of a high horse. Once you get up there, the height of it makes you giddy and reluctant to shut up.

And why draw on a pig when there are people? So many people with so much skin, such blank and wide expanses of it, to be etched on, to be coloured in.

Uncle Mark would really like to yell at me and make me see his point, I think, but he cannot do that because I could open my mouth again and start to say things and never ever stop. There are so many little moments I could tell of, so many things. It's hard to prove a rape – it comes down to woman against man. After a while we talk about it as if it was a thing. That I could tell. People. That he could maybe pay for what he did. They put people away. Mark and Claire and Susan would take the case, but I would be a witness or something like that. We have to talk to guards, and sort it out. See what our options are.

There are so many things you can do to a person who says yes, and that they want it.

He only left her with him for an afternoon, when Claire was out at training. He wanted to get some stuff done at the office. And everything seemed to be OK so he did it all over again. The same thing. 'I mean, the man was family. My brother.'

He knew that something was wrong with Dad and us, the way he cowed Mam down, but he didn't know about me. And the way he says it makes me feel as though it is my fault that he hurt Susan. I should have screamed and screamed and made good and sure that everybody heard me. That they knew, at least that there was the question.

That there was smoke and that there could be fire. I mean, it is a horrid thing to say about somebody. Unless it's true. And it is true, but it is still horrible to say.

People choose so many painful things. Ink me. Pierce me. Split my tongue. Put needles in my face. Leave scars on me but make them really artful. Hurt me in the prettiest of ways. Stay with me. I know that you don't love me but please stay.

Susan is so tough. She is a tubby little thing with wispy hair. She climbs things and kicks balls and yells things to her brother across the room and doesn't give a toss. I kind of love her attitude. I'd hate to see it killed in her. What possessed Dad to think he could make her keep a secret? I suppose he got away with lots before. Once you do something once, maybe it gets easier to do. I worry sometimes when I get tattoos I'll end up covered, becoming an enormous painted lady, like that tiger-woman or the fellow in New Zealand who is covered in thick, oily looking scales and has had his tongue split in two as well.

Tongue-splitting is a thing I can't imagine why people would want to do. Why would you want a forked tongue like a demon or a snake when you could have an unsplit person's tongue that doesn't sort of brand you as a liar. It does not creep me out once it is done, but after it is done, then the muscle has healed and it can move and wrap around itself, like little legs. You forget the tongue is a muscle. In your everyday life there is not much call for it to be thought of as such. It helps you talk, which doesn't take much effort.

Braid my hair, put boobs inside my boobs to make them bigger, draw circles under eyes and eyebrows over. Draw on me and fill me. Make me pretty. Make me feel I'm prettier than now. Or scarier. Or cooler. I want to be more how I want to be. The way I want to feel inside is how I want to look to other people. Hurt me. Make that happen. Fix it all.

Uncle Mark and Mam and Gran and me are eating dinner, which is kind of nice. The family together. Gran has got a new parish priest, and she doesn't like him as much as the old one, who had been there twenty years and was a friend of hers – he married Mam and Dad. Which isn't to say he's not a pleasant man, someone had to marry them, I suppose. He is moving to a city parish and he doesn't want to. His last mass was the saddest thing that Gran had ever seen. 'He was very close to tears,' Gran says, and shakes her head in what seems like pity, or something wistful anyway.

I think for her priests are the same as counsellors. And she suddenly has plenty to consider telling someone. I remember when anybody mentioned child abuse in Ireland, she was very sympathetic to the church, she kind of said it did not happen to everyone, and it was sad, but it was not the church's fault at all. I wonder if she is wondering if that is why God gave her this burden. That it would be one she might have needed to carry. If I am to be reduced to some sort of cosmic lesson.

The Sky Bear would not meddle in the lives of silly men and silly women. All his lessons would be bear-related, like how Rupert would not have needed a scarf, with his thick white pelt, or how Winnie-the-Pooh was a bit wet and useless or else he would have eaten Piglet ages ago. Roasted him in honey like a hero and then roared a bearish roar.

That is the kind of thing I could relate to. If I were a bear, I'd eat my friends – if they were pigs. Or cows. Or sheep. Or humans who came too near my cubs. If I were a bear I would have cubs. I don't want human babies. They are too much effort. With a cub you only really give it six months or so and then it is alright. With humans it is different. We are so soft and have so much to learn.

I own a lot of make-up. I don't wear it. But I own it. Stuff I've gotten free with magazines. You send them back but you get to keep the free gifts sometimes. Depending on who's working with you. Stuff I've bought with vouchers, borrowed from my friends or from Mam and never given back. It's all the same thing. Changing who you are. A face upon your face so people want to have you.

It is very hard to tell someone *No* when you are very small. Susan didn't say a thing at first, he said it was a secret and if she kept the secret for a week, he would give her a present. The second time, he tried to make her do more stuff, and she was very brave and she yelled, 'NO!' and locked herself in the bathroom. He pretended he had no idea why, but he really did. When Claire came home, she told her what had happened. She would have told Uncle Mark but he came home last. Claire is really angry with my dad. And so is Uncle Mark and so is Gran.

If you get a spot you use primer and concealer and foundation and then you have a bump that is the same colour as the rest of your skin. I always dug, though. I am such a picker I can't help it.

We all eat our lasagne up after a while. It is nice, even if I do say so myself. I put kidney beans and little slices of rasher without the fat into the mince to make it a bit more special. Over the meal, Gran says that I should start to go to mass, that it would make me feel better about it. Calm my troubled soul. I tell her that I'm not sure that I believe in God. She says, 'You're in despair and I can see why, but He will wait for you.'

I tell her, 'It would feel weird to pray to a Father after what mine did to me, though, wouldn't it?'

She shuts up.

I am glad that they are staying in a hotel. We don't have room for them here and it would be weird to have them around. We need to talk about them once they're gone. The hotel that they're staying in has a pool. Tomorrow, Gran wants to take me swimming after work. I tell her that sounds lovely. It kind of does, but it is hard to imagine Gran in a bathing suit. Maybe one of those Victorian ones that goes down to the knees. She does aqua-aerobics in the centre near her house. Isn't that strange? Mam catches my eye when she talks about it and her eyes are full of amusement, not laughing at Gran or anything, but it seems such an incongruous thing for her to do. Although she can do anything, my gran. All these courses with the ICA before her hands. Basket-weaving, quilting till her hands were sore, then baking with a mixer, painting, hill-walks.

It's not her ability that surprises me. It's her exposing skin. I've only ever seen her fully clothed. Except for in the hospital – and even then, pyjamas buttoned right up to the neck and looking put together. She almost died when I was ten. Maybe she should have. Like Granny

Kate, she wouldn't have to know about the kind of family we were. I'm trying to be kind to Gran and Mark now. It's a thing. I've thought about it for a while and even though they aren't very good at being family, or weren't for a while, they're kind of all I have, and if I get them back I'll have an option if things with Mam get wobblier at all. You kind of have to be a bit strategic. It doesn't mean I'll trust them, like. It doesn't.

You have to be conscious of how other people perceive you. If you don't make an effort or make too much of one it can stick out. You want to stick out for the better reasons. I draw a swallow, pierced with a dagger. I draw a little hand that holds a heart. Hands are hard to draw properly, they keep going a little bit like claws. Cats can suck the claws back in their pads when they are being gentle. There's only one they can't retract. A spur.

I am working from seven till two tomorrow, even though I'm still quite sick. It is usually pretty quiet on Sundays. Mostly it is tidying and organising things, restocking and so on. Making pre-packed sandwiches. It is amazing how many people buy pre-packed sandwiches when we make them up with fresh stuff in front of them for the exact same price. Maybe I should put my number up for babysitting, now that I don't need the nights for occasional Tom. Maybe I could afford some new inks soon, if I made a bit more money. And I could do my homework while the kiddies slept.

Uncle Mark offers to do the wash up and Gran says, 'Don't be silly,' at the same time as Mam says, 'That would be nice, thanks.' So he does. Gran helps him, and then we watch the news. Nothing much is happening in the world. I mean, the politicians are worried about something, but it's not a war or a famine or whatever so that's always a nice bonus. We are so little with our little problems. But today felt big.

When Gran leaves she gives me a fabricky hug.

Swimming with my gran tomorrow. How weird! I haven't been swimming in ages. I can swim. I learned how when I was small in school – we used to go once a week for about ten weeks a year. When I got older, though, it felt too much like showing off my body. What people could see. The paleness of my skin, bits of stubble missed while shaving legs or pits.

Cats groom themselves out in the open, though. We hide it. Sort of.

After they left, Mam asked me to bring the plates over to Tom's. I want to tell her where to go but I am nosy so I drop them over. He answers the door, but doesn't ask me in. I thank him for the plates, and turn to go. He says to wait and asks if I'm OK. I say: 'I am. And you?'

He says he thinks that he might miss me.

'What about the girl?' I ask, and wait for him to say something that matters.

He doesn't. He just wants someone to bone. I can tell by the look on his face, the puppy-dog one he thinks is sexy but is really just pathetic and cute. He shakes his head and asks me, 'Do you miss me?'

I tell him I'll survive. He will too, but it's nice to know he still wants me a bit. I would like to have some physical affection and I do not want to think, but instead I go back home and shave my legs twice in a shower that goes cold after the first ten minutes.

I come back downstairs in my dressing gown, pyjamas and towel-turban wrapped around my hair. Mam is boiling the kettle for tea but she lets me have the water for my hot-water bottle which is really nice. She says she wasn't expecting all the things that Gran and Uncle Mark said, and what did I think of it all?

I say, 'I need to sleep on it, I think I've done enough talking for one day.' My brain feels like it has been wrung out, like we do with hand-wash-only tops. Mam says she feels wrecked as well, but cannot get her mind to fall asleep. She is going to stay up watching a tacky romantic comedy and drinking wine to try and wear herself out.

I do not ask her what happened with Simon. She did not mention him at all, all day, and normally her talk is peppered with little references to him, opinions that he has, his anecdotes and quirks. I don't know what happened, if they've broken up or had a fight or something else.

I have a lot of things to think about, but instead of thinking about them, I brush my hair out, dry it straight enough and listen to my Walkman as I go to bed. All songs are love songs, at least in my collection. It is strange how important love is to artists. I wish someone would release an album filled with simple pleasures that have nothing to do with the person they fancy. Like the joy of cleaning the house and having it be perfect for ten minutes before someone comes and messes it up. Or when you have a spot on your forehead and it's all you can think about and one day it goes away and it is as if it was never there and you do not think about it ever again, and nobody can tell that once there was a spot on that piece of skin which is so smooth right now. Or about all the different types of tattoo people get. Stupid humans, liking other humans instead of things they can and can't control.

You could make a thing of all that grooming, if you wanted. Put pretty packaging, polishes and fat yellow 1950s hairdryers, lipsticks, compacts, eyelashes and sequins down an arm. The other could be tampons, dirty cotton wool, razors with hair clinging to them. Toilets. Two sleeves. One fancy, one disgusting. But thematically linked like poems they make us study.

I take the polish off my nails and paint them all over again. My toenails too. They are a dark dark purple, almost black now with a high-gloss top coat that really makes them shine. Sleep will crease them, work will chip them, but at least I made the effort. I fall asleep and when I do I dream that I am slowly washing Susan's wispy blondish hair. She is really wide-eyed and quiet, looking up at me as I massage the shampoo in. I rinse it out, holding my hand like a visor over her eye so the suds don't get in. I never liked it when the suds got in my eyes when I was small. When this is done I dry her hair roughly with a towel and then brush it out gently and begin to run my fingers through it. My fingernails are scissors and even though I do not want to I end up cutting most of her hair off. Her face is calm, her head as round and white as the moon.

'Why are you doing this to me?' she asks. 'Why are you doing this to me?'

I wish I was a crow to fly right out the window and escape back to a nest I share with no-one. But I am not a crow and so I start to sob. When I reach up to dry my tears, I realise that I, too, am hairless. Not even eyelashes do I possess. It is so strange I almost forget why I am sad. I blink and hold my eyes shut for an age, squeezing them tight, it is the first time I ever remember purposely closing my eyes inside a dream. When I open them, Susan is gone. Her hair litters the floor like straw and I can't spin it into gold. Even if I had the necessary skills I have no spindle. All that broken hair made me sad. And then I don't remember any more.

There are things you can do elegantly in front of people. Get drawn on, put on lipstick or mascara. Eye and lip emphasising things, things that show you're cool. You don't show people washing off the ooze or changing dressings. You don't show people most of what it takes to be a person.

A CAPSULE OF YOUR YOUNGER ADULT SELF

She has the bluest face, my sexy zombie. She has a hula skirt and she is winking. The notebook that I got when I moved here is almost full. I wonder where I find the time to do it. Gouged it out of sleep or stole it from other things. Hula girls and sailor patterns. What would I do, if I could draw on family and friends?

Morning wakes me, streaming through the window, climbing in my ears and whistling loudly. Six AM is not officially morning. It is a time to go home, not to wake up. I dress in jeans and my polo shirt. Big fluffy cardigan over it to stave off the cold that creeps into your bones when you have to spend quality time with refrigerated items. I get to work at quarter to, Katrina's not there yet and she has the keys, she comes at seven, by which time I have died of hypothermia. The first thing that she says to me is that there is a nip in it. I nod at her. Of course there is, you bitch. She laughs, opens up the shop and types in the security code. I take the papers in, and sort them out, then I restock all the stuff that they faced off last night.

Friday is a big night out for the employees here. Also Saturday. They all get locked and hook up with each other. It is bad to work the mornings after because sometimes they start drinking at work and leave the place a tip. It is good for gossip, though, and for having something to talk about, but not be too involved in. I rarely join them, being underage and only part-time and constantly broke and all. Katrina is talking about where they went and what they did and I don't really care, but it passes the time, having something to talk about. Like storytime to distract me from my thoughts of how strange and hard it would be if I do what Uncle Mark probably wants me to do.

He hasn't really done his homework on it. I mean, he wasn't even able to tell me how much out of my life it would take. If I turn eighteen before it goes to court, if it even does, do I still get to be anonymous? Because papers love stories about people who go through horrible stuff, even more so if there's a sex-abuse angle.

I hate seeing those faces in the bookshops, big wide eyes on white backgrounds and titles like 'Please Daddy Stop' or 'Why Mummy Why?' Parents everywhere are abusing children everywhere, they seem to say to me, and it doesn't make me feel less alone, just way more hopeless about the world we live in. I mean, if it's a genre. If people like to read about it. I mean, who likes to read about that kind of thing? It's people's private pain. Stories that are real are not any more interesting but the fact that they are, like, a thing feels very wrong. Like sniffing someone's panties. That level of creepy.

Someone cheated on his girlfriend with someone else and I'm supposed to care. I shake my head and say that I don't really understand why men have so much trouble being faithful. Like Tom (maybe) and my dad. Not that I wanted Dad to be faithful or anything. I just wanted him to go away.

I'd love if he got cancer, but he would probably want to be minded by his family, Gran and Mam and Uncle Mark and all the rest. I wonder how doomed he would have to be before they forgave him?

I don't think Uncle Mark ever would. Claire wouldn't let him for one thing. But would Mam? I mean, I know she didn't strictly know or whatever, but I suspect that she suspected something, and she was so angry when she found out about the affair. Which is strange, because it's not like she fancied him any more, or that he was even decent to her. But apparently, her marriage vows still meant something. She was more visibly angry about that than she was about the other. Fair enough, it is an easier one to talk about, but I could have done with a bit more unadulterated rage. I would have liked my mam to fight my corner a bit more. To throw acid in his face, flay him. Drug him and drive his car over a cliff. Hobble him and starve him to a drawn-out demise, until he resembled a handbag made of skin and full of bones.

Or love me enough for me to be enough, to want to focus on me, make it up to me, make the effort. Not to keep on being sad, because we should be happy now and I am trying, I am trying so, so hard. I sometimes wish I had a different mam, because then maybe I would be different, stronger, healthier inside my mind and soul.

For Mam, a little lion to be brave. Or a keyhole and a key for escape. The lion just beneath her armpit, the tiny key and keyhole on her wrists. They'd have to be small, for Mam. She's not that brave, for all I'd give her lions. I could see her fainting halfway through.

It is weird how many people buy tinned peas. I am always having to re-stock them. I hate the taste – they're like the grossest thing. I would rather drink a pint of dishwater than eat a tin of those. We turn the lights on and open up. I slice some ham. It makes a noise like a pig giving birth and shudders to a crunching halt. I jump back from it as though it had tried to bite me. I tell Kat

I think that it is broken and she says to just use packaged ham until she phones the manager to get it fixed. She says she is scared of the ham-slicer, she doesn't like to use it. She is vegetarian and isn't a fan of meat products at all, she hates to handle them or smell them. She says it sounds like it growls at her, it makes her neck hair go all funny.

She has short hair, Katrina, and it goes down her nape in a kind of a triangle. I sometimes think about cutting my hair short-short, a clean kind of cut that I would never have to worry about minding. I'd shake my head to dry it after showers like a dog. I don't know, though, it's such a big decision. I like my curtain of hair. It's great for not catching people's eyes at school and one of my favourite feelings is when the wind blows it from my face all the way back, just perfectly. I feel all cheekbones and wisps then, like an elf or an alien princess. A girl in a film, who could be anyone but isn't anyone. Normal and special, just like everyone else and not at all. Maybe my boy-next-door would love me then, if I could be that girl, in the wind the whole time. Instead of just on days with a certain type of quite specific weather.

It's really only me and Mam for family. I don't have friends I'm close enough to to call them that, and Mark and Gran are back but they are new. I do not really trust them. Maybe a snake for Mark, you know the one, the black one eating the

white one. Or it's own tail maybe. Things that go in circles.
What goes around comes around. He'd like something with
Justice at the moment I reckon. I don't know if I can give
him that or help with it. It is a lot to ask. He should let me
tattoo him as a bribe. The snake would go in the centre of
his back, and so would justice. I feel it would be one or the
other with him.

My hands have newsprint on them, even though I've
washed them. It looks gross. I try and try to scrub them
clean but I can't, so I just wear plastic gloves, the last
thing that people want is someone making food for
them with the hands of a homeless person.

Not that all homeless people are dirty or anything. I
mean, I could easily be homeless, I wouldn't rule it out
just yet or anything. All it takes is a bigger row with
Mam than usual, or one of us to lose our job. Another
fuck-up in the long line of previous fuck-ups that have
led us to this place where we live now, so I cannot really
judge. Where would you shower if you were homeless,
though? Where would you wash? Maybe in the pool,
but you would need togs and things and shampoo and
conditioner. I wonder where those people leave their
stuff, the logistics of it are kind of hard to fathom. I've
always had a roof over my head. I would be scared if I

had to sleep on streets, because strangers can be horrible as well. Men especially, but also other women.

Anyway, I do not like having dirty hands. Thank God for my purple nail polish. There's nothing worse than dirty, filthy nails.

Wafer-thin honey ham is the cheapest ham we have, so we use that. Some people come in for breakfast rolls, which is strange, because, apart from us, who has to work this early on a Sunday? By nine o'clock we are busy with people, though – papers and croissants, hangover food and food for people who are not hungover but are still hungry. Winos who want drink, but cannot get served any drink till noon. They eye the clock hungrily. The classy ones who do not look like winos normally wait till after noon and buy food as well so it does not look overly suspicious. You wouldn't know to look at people how much they depend on stupid things like drink and smokes and chocolate and scratch cards. I wonder what I would run to the shop for in my pyjamas. Maybe milk.

I like to work on Sundays because the pay is better and you get to take home all the papers. We never sell them all so I get an enormous sheaf of supplements to keep me going for the week ahead. It's nice to get things free. I cut out illustrations that I like from them and stick them in this scrapbook that I have, I use it for ideas for my sketchbook. Not that I copy them directly.

Except I sometimes do. You have to be able to because people want really specific things – sketches from da Vinci to be copied, particular cartoon characters. And if you copy, you better do it well. There's nothing like a bad copy of a thing you love to depress you. A tattoo of Mickey Mouse is lame, but a tattoo of Mickey Mouse that only vaguely looks like Mickey Mouse is fucking heartbreaking.

Katrina has a tramp stamp on her back, it is a kind of woven Celtic web. She got it back when she lived in Poland. She says her friend was getting one and she got one as well to keep her company. It doesn't look that great. The design is complicated but kind of bland and the dark has faded quite a bit. It's not the kind of thing you'd want to show off.

It is harder to get a tattoo removed than to get a tattoo in the first place. Also it's more painful. You can get a lot of things corrected if only you have money. I know it can't buy happiness, but it can buy security and at least that's something. It would be comforting to be secure, to know that you were going to be OK no matter how bad things got, that you would eat and have somewhere to sleep. That you could get a really good education and never ever have to use it. It would be amazing to be wealthy, to be proper heiress-rich. To not have to clean the employee toilets in the lull because it is my turn.

My stomach hurts and the chemicals make my head feel all weird. I should probably eat some sort of breakfast thing. I haven't had a bite since the lasagne yesterday. The crumble lingers untouched in the fridge. I'll eat it tonight. And watch romantic comedies. But wait, there is my homework. Urrgh. I totally forgot about my homework. I wonder if Mam could write me a note to say that I was sick (true) or had family things going on (truer). She might, if I catch her in the right mood.

The last thing I want to do today is trigonometry. The second last is swimming-fun with Gran.

What would Gran have? Classy things. Pearls. An elegant biblical quote. A single flower. Not a rose. A hydrangea or peony perhaps. Fat blue blooms that cluster soft, acidic on her shoulder. Gran is sharp. She likes to grow hydrangeas.

Gran picks me up in her car after work. She has bought me a swimsuit. It is black with purple at the sides. There is a hat that doesn't really match. In the hotel pool, you have to wear a hat. We don't talk about yesterday at all, really. She drives and asks me about my plans for college. I tell her I don't know. That money is tight. She tells me not to worry about money, that she has quite a tidy sum put by and would rather use it while she's still alive. I tell her, 'I'll manage,' and she says it is the least that she could do, and not that it would take away what happened and the things she should have done, but maybe it would help a little now, to make my life more comfortable and that is really all that she would want. I don't know how to answer her, so I tell her I'd like to study art. She says she's not surprised. When I was little I remembered pictures more than stories. When she'd read me books, I'd always doodle in the margins of my copies.

'I still do that,' I tell her, and she smiles.

It would feel weird to stab into my gran or mam or uncle. Satisfying, though, I would imagine.

In the hotel, we go down to the basement, where the pool is. It's blue and white like every pool ever, and as I go through the little metal gate to it I'm warm. The chlorine smell is nice. It reminds me of being small. The happy kind of small, where you are minded and taken different places.

'I haven't swum in years,' I tell her soft.

We change in separate cubicles, adjoining. Gran looks trim in her dark and light blue tankini.

'It's a top and little shorts,' she says. 'I like it because when you're old you don't want to be showing off your body.'

I smile at her. I tell her she looks great. I think I mean

it. She touches me and says that I'm a 'great girl' and I think she almost tells me she is sorry but she doesn't. I can see the thin blue veins threading under her skin, pale as parchment weaving in and out. The colours there are intricate and lovely. It takes so much to keep a person going, so many things click in to make it right. Every bit of us is body art, stuck together with flesh and who we are. My head hurts when I think of how many people there are in the world. Sometimes in a scared way, sometimes not.

A little brown bird. A sparrow. Something light and feathered, perching on my shoulder just for hope.

I swim along the lanes, front crawl, arms circling, head tilted to the side and gulping air. Gran is quick, but I am young and quicker. I think about the offer to help with college. I know it's kind of paying off her guilt, but I would rather ease her guilt than Dad's. Not that he feels any. But still.

I think about leaving Mam. I think about pictures.

The elastic of the swimming cap bites into my forehead. I swim up and down and up and down till I forget things. My stuffed up nose is throbbing. Up and down and up and down until I grab the wall and grasp it tight and breathe as though it's food and I am hungry, starving.

And if they change their mind – or I change mine – here's the thing. It isn't quite for ever. Tattoos can be removed – they burn them off. It is a painful process and expensive. But it happens. Something that's a part of you, singed and worked on, until it is no longer even there. The memory of pain. And just a scar.